THE LIBRARIAN

The Goblin Archives

CIARA GRAVES

The Librarian
THE GOBLIN ARCHIVES BOOK ONE

Portland, Oregon.

Nienna Havard. College student. Librarian. No one special. She's keeping a secret. Her mother's in an mental institution after vanishing for several years. She came back talking about elves, goblins, and wars.

To compound matters, she's having a hard time breaking up with the guy who clearly isn't right for her. Or maybe she's not right for him. Either way, she can't figure out how to tell him that they aren't working out.

Alred Lightvale. Elf. Hot. Protector of the Historian. He traveled to the human world to find a girl who's supposed to replace the recently murdered Historian. He's got a tight timeline to get the next Historian in place.

One problem. She's not exactly buying it. And she sure as heck isn't interested in joining the cause.

A speeding arrow embedded in the trunk of a tree as I kicked my horse, urging him on faster.

The shrieking of the goblin warband gained on me. Cursing, I guided my horse sharply to the right, ducking under low hanging branches, racing to get back to camp. When torch lights came into view, I grabbed the horn at my waist and pressed it to my lips, signaling the guards.

My call was cut short when an arrow embedded in my right shoulder, jerking me forward. I glared at the encroaching enemy. The camp was just ahead. I rode by the guards already falling in line to meet the attack.

"Alred!"

I spun my steed around, grunting at my latest injury, and slipped from the saddle as Jurgis hurried forward. "Where is he?"

"He's here, and he's been asking for you. Where were you?"

"Where do you think?" I snapped, gripping my right arm. "They've surrounded us. We have no way back to the Council now. I sent a raven for reinforcements, but they won't be here for hours. The goblins have set up barricades along the main roads. They've come for him."

"We don't have hours." Jurgis wrung his hands, his long blond hair falling over his face. He shoved it out of the way, rushing behind me to deal with the arrow jutting out of my shoulder. Without warning, he yanked it free. When he started to remove my leather overcoat, I shoved his hands away.

"I'll live. Now tell me what happened." I demanded. "Jurgis!"

"Sorry, right. He should have told you. I urged him to, but you know how he is, and now it's too late. It's too damned late." His bright blue eyes filled with grief.

I stormed around him, headed for the crimson tent in the center.

"Alred, wait."

"No. I could've prevented all of this." At least now, the goblins' sudden urge to attack us made sense. I stomped to the tent and threw back the canvas. "What in all the gods' names do you think you're doing?"

"Ah, Alred, you've returned, and just in time, it sounds like."

I glowered at Garrick Havard, the elf that had been under my charge for the last twenty-seven years here in Kenzu'grote. "Why?"

Garrick's brow rose, but he didn't look up from the heavy tome he currently wrote in. "I don't think I need to answer that question. Not exactly something you bring up during polite conversation."

"How long have you known?"

"Two days."

If I hadn't just been shot with an arrow, I'd be strangling the elf. "I'm your Protector, remember? You are supposed to tell me so I can keep you alive."

"But this isn't about you keeping me alive, not now. You and I both know how this works."

"That's not the point. I could've moved you, and this goblin war band wouldn't be charging toward us," I argued, though deep down, I knew he was right. Giving up wasn't in me, however. "There's still time. Get your ass on your horse. I'll find us a path to safety."

"No."

I ground my teeth. "Just like that? You're giving up?"

Garrick continued to write until he reached the very end of the very last page. He nodded as if satisfied with what he'd accomplished and set the quill aside. He sprinkled sand on the ink then blew on the page as he had done so many times before over the decades. Leaving the tome open, he stood and came toward me, a sad smile on his face.

"Once you've returned to the Seven, they will need to see those final pages," he said.

"You can show them yourself," I countered.

That sad smile was fixed on his lips.

I ran a hand down my face, not ready to accept what was about to happen. "You are giving up. How can you do this? You were so close to fixing everything."

"That is now a job for the next Historian. You must find her before they do."

"Garrick," I tried, but he rested his hands on my shoulders, eyes narrowed.

"You find her, Alred, and you keep her safe, you understand me? You protect her as you protected me." He swallowed hard and backed away. "She doesn't know anything about our world. You'll have to teach her."

"I'm not a teacher," I reminded him.

"You are now. She'll be like no Historian before her. She'll need guidance and a friend, much as you have been for me." Another horn blew as the goblin war band closed in. "My time has come, and so has yours."

"I'm not leaving you until it's over."

"I'm not giving you a choice. You served me well, Alred Lightvale. Now it's time for you to serve another."

I studied the elf's face, hating how unfair life was. He'd barely reached his prime in elf years, and his end was here. His dark red hair was run through with several white strands, but otherwise, there was no way to tell he was more than two hundred and twenty years old. I was at a loss for what to say. I'd been warned this moment would come, but never thought it'd be this soon.

"It was an honor to have served you," I replied finally, bowing and crossing my left arm over my chest. "But I'm staying with you until the bitter end."

Garrick pulled a small, glass jar from his pocket, shaking his head. "Not this time, friend."

He threw it at the tent wall, and the jar exploded, creating a swirling portal of dark cobalt and emerald light. He gathered the tome off the table, closed it, and handed it to me. I was a much larger and stronger elf than Garrick and planned to stay until a goblin shrieked right outside his tent.

I turned, reaching for my sword when Garrick shoved me hard. I shouted as I was sucked into the portal. The last thing I saw before the lights faded was Garrick drawing his sword and letting out a battle cry, meeting his death head-on.

The portal closed with a loud pop even as I lunged to my feet, desperate to get back.

"Bastard."

I gripped the hilt of my sword, not entirely sure what I was going to do with it yet. I couldn't get back in time to save him, not now. The only way to return to Kenzu'grote was to find one of the hidden doors, since he hadn't been kind enough to send me with another portal to return. He knew me too well. I would've already been back at his side, fighting.

A quick glance told me I was nowhere near one of the few doorways that existed between worlds. Swearing under my breath, I started to draw my sword, but shoved it viciously in its sheath and looked for the tome Garrick had given me. The massive volume rested on the grass a few feet away, unharmed.

I swiped my hand over the leather cover and hoisted it into my arms. Thankfully, the book began to shrink in size until it fit in my palm. I tucked it in the leather pouch at my hip, under my overcoat, letting out a breath to temper my anger. With Garrick gone, it was now my duty to find the next Historian. There would be a chance to grieve his death later, but now, time was not on my side.

I wasn't going to be the only one searching for the clueless Historian.

Music blared somewhere ahead of me through the trees. I glared into the darkness.

Humans.

I hated their world. It was far too noisy, and there were too many damned people everywhere. Fumbling in another pocket of my coat, I removed the small, antique silver compass that never pointed north. Shutting my eyes, I held it steady in my palm and waited. Clearing my mind, I centered my thoughts on finding the one I sought.

In the history of the elves since the first Historian came into being, Historians had always been elves. Garrick had changed everything when he fell in love with a human woman. He'd never imagined his daughter from that union would be the one to take his place, but that was who the tome called out to and whose face was shown to him as his successor. There was no changing who it was destined to be.

I squinted an eye open to see the needle in the compass hadn't budged. Sighing, I shut my eyes and concentrated harder on what I pursued. The new Historian was a half-blood. The usual tracking methods might not work. If I had known what she looked like, where she lived, I could have simply tracked her down. But I didn't. Garrick never had pictures of his daughter, and I hadn't seen her the last few times we traveled between realms. I was almost ready to track her down the non-magic way when the compass warmed.

I opened my eyes to find it pointing northeast. I started to walk forward until I remembered humans weren't accustomed to seeing someone bearing a sword. It wasn't as if a goblin war band was going to come around the corner, not here.

Not yet, at least.

I removed my overcoat and adjusted my short sword, so it hung on my back instead, the hilt hidden by my hood when I put my coat back on. The dagger at my left wasn't noticeable. I put the compass in my palm and set off to find Garrick's daughter and the next Historian.

***

Another group of students gawked as they walked by, and I pointedly glared until their eyes widened, and they scurried away like frightened rats. For two days, I'd been stalking the campus of Higgins University of Portland, observing the woman the compass was leading me to. And for two days, I'd prayed it was wrong. Garrick had warned me she would know nothing of this world. I couldn't lie, I hoped for someone a bit more, well, not Nienna.

The first day I spotted her, I willed the compass to guide me to someone else. I'd watched as she walked with some human named Phil on the first day. He'd draped his arm around her shoulders as they laughed about something on their phones. He had prevented me from getting close to Nienna, giving me more time to observe my new charge.

The Goblin Historian was tasked with archiving the histories of the wars, in a sense. It was true they spent most of their time seeing and writing, but they had to learn to fight as well. Had to learn to defend themselves. It was not the life for a soft person—an innocent. After two days, it was clear the only thing Nienna knew how to wield was a book.

From all I'd witnessed, she spent her days in classrooms, and when she wasn't there, she was in the library, burying her face in books, or working behind the large desk. I sat on a bench beneath a tree today, waiting to catch a glimpse of her leaving the library. I had yet to come up with a way to approach her that wouldn't scare her off.

She'd grown up in a world without magic or fear of goblins. She'd grown up not knowing who her father was, or what she might become. My going up to her and announcing who I was and where I came from might not go over so well.

"Is there a comic-con in town?"

I glanced to find three humans sniggering as they stared at me. I ignored them and went back to searching for Nienna, but they stayed put.

"Check out those ears, man. Hey, I know, he was born with those, and this is how he fits in."

"Are you quite finished?" I asked sharply.

"It speaks! Hey, can you take us to destroy the ring?" the third one said through his laughter as he was high-fived.

In one quick move, I was off the bench and had knocked into the humans with my full weight, sending them to the ground. I hauled the middle one up by his shirt, smirking when his feet dangled pathetically above the sidewalk. The other two remained on the ground, staring at me, confused.

"I suggest you keep your mocking to your-selves," I warned, "or you'll see what else I have aside from pointed ears." I dropped the human, and he landed hard on his rump. His friends didn't wait for him, but took off, leaving him to run after them, tripping twice on his way. I shook my head and resumed my seat on the bench.

A brief glance at my attire had me wondering if I shouldn't find clothes to fit in better, but a flash of reddish-blond—more blond than red—hair caught my eye. Nienna. She was alone today, holding a stack of books in her arms as she strode across the grass. The top book was open, her lips moving as she read, I presumed. I moved with her, keeping my distance. Sunlight brought out the various hues of red in her hair, reminding me of changing leaves in autumn, blowing in the breeze. Freckles dotted her cheeks. Dark jeans hugged her legs, and black boots reached her knees, giving her an extra few inches of height. The forest green sweater she wore hung off her right shoulder, and I found my gaze lingering there until I dragged it away, not sure why I cared what she wore in the first place. None of it was fit for life in Kenzu'grote. Her gaze flicked up swiftly, then back down, and I glimpsed the bright green eyes that were so like Garrick's that for a moment, I forgot where I was.

A sharp pain of loss and anger stabbed at me, and I shook my head, reminding myself of my oath.

In the few seconds I looked away, Nienna shifted course and headed straight for me. I should've moved out of her way, but my boots remained planted in the grass. Here, with so many witnesses, was probably not the time to tell her of her calling, but I had to do it soon. I was about to retreat to the shadows of the nearby building when a guy called out. A football flew toward Nienna.

At the last second, I stretched out a hand and caught the ball.

Nienna's head jerked up, and the books toppled to the ground. I tossed the ball back to the human and bent to help her pick them up.

"Shit," she muttered, gingerly lifting two of the books and closing them. "Don't be damaged. Please don't be damaged." She sighed in relief, running her fingers over the spines.

Her care for the inanimate objects baffled me. "You should pay attention to your surroundings," I commented, figuring now was a good a time as any to start her lessons.

Her hands stilled, and she looked up, laughing. The sound was full of life and happiness. A small part of me hated that I would be stealing that away from her. If the life her father and I had led had one guarantee, it was that happiness was nearly impossible to find and hold onto. "Yeah, I probably should," she said, her smile crooked. A dimple appeared in her right cheek, and I fumbled with the books in my hands. "Thanks, by the way. Saved me from getting smoked in the head."

My brow furrowed, and I handed her the rest of her books. "Yes, well, as I said—"

"Pay attention to my surroundings," she finished for me. "Got it." With books in hand, she stood, giving me a quizzical once-over. "Damn, that is a nice costume. I'm extremely jealous. Are you part of the fair?"

"The fair?" I asked, doing my best to hide my annoyance.

"Yeah, the renaissance fair? You look incredible. It all looks so real and worn." She reached for my arm, raising it as she inspected the leather bracer. "This detail must've taken you forever to get right. Did you make all this yourself?"

"Ah, no, but I maintain it," I said quietly.

"Huh. You'll have to tell me where you get your stuff. I always want to dress up, but there's never time." She checked the silver watch on her wrist.

It wasn't the watch that made me stiffen. Sunlight glinted off the gold thick-banded bracelet above her watch. I recognized it as the one Garrick had crafted for her. The band bore an enchantment, but I sensed Nienna had no idea she was being affected by magic. I doubt she believed magic existed.

"Hey, you okay?"

"Yes, quite." I stepped to the side with a polite smile. "I don't want to keep you waiting if you have somewhere you have to be."

"I do, sadly. Uh, I work in the library if you want to continue this conversation. I'm there almost every night." She twisted her lips to the side, bouncing on the balls of her feet, seeming to debate staying to talk with me.

"Nienna!"

I bit back a grunt.

The human called Phil had yelled for her. Our conversation would have to wait. Why couldn't she have been in Kenzu'grote already? The tome's call would've reached her there, and she would've come to me instead of the other way around.

"I guess I'll see you around?" she asked after she waved across the way to Phil.

"Yes, I'm sure you will." I smiled and started to bow and cross my left arm over my chest, stopping myself just in time. "It was very nice to meet you, Nienna."

"And you…" She trailed off, and I told her my name. "Alred. I like that. See you around."

Clasping my hands behind my back, I watched her go.

Phil took half the stack of books from her and kissed her cheek.

I bristled at the action. I was taking her away from more than just her job and her schooling. I'd be stealing her away from a possible love. It was rare for a Protector or Historian to have a relationship of any kind. Very few had managed to. Garrick was one of the lucky ones. But not me, not ever. There was no point when my job was literally my life.

"Tomorrow," I whispered. "You'll tell her everything tomorrow."

Chapter 2
NIENNA

Rain pattered the window in the lobby as I waited to sign in to visit Mom. Another rainy day in Portland was nothing new. Since yesterday, all I kept thinking about was that Alred guy on campus. There'd been something about him that made me want to keep talking to him. When he hadn't appeared in the library last night, I admitted to myself I was disappointed. I fiddled with my black crossbody purse, wondering if he'd show up today, though I wasn't sure why I wanted to see him again.

"He was just some guy, and you have enough going on in your life. And Phil. You have Phil. Remember Phil," I muttered aloud, but my words did nothing to make me feel better. For weeks, I'd meant to talk to Phil about us, but each time, I'd chickened out. "You'll do it today."

"Uh, Nienna? You okay over there?"

I jumped, turning to find Harry, one of my Mom's doctors, giving me a curious glance. I hadn't even heard him approach. "Yeah, just you know, thinking aloud."

"About Phil."

"Yep."

"You know, this isn't really the place to be caught talking to yourself," he said, motioning to the psych ward sign over his head.

I cringed. "Good point. How is she today?" I asked, following him through a set of double doors.

We came out in a short hall and had to be buzzed in through another set of doors by the security guard sitting to our right. Harry held the door open for me and joined me as we walked a familiar path through the old, stone monastery that had been converted into a home for the mentally ill.

The halls were lined with tall, narrow windows overlooking a central courtyard. Paths crisscrossed the bright green grass and bordered vibrant gardens filled with tulips, lilies, and other flowers the residents helped plant and maintain. A fountain sat in the very heart of the courtyard, flowing peacefully into a large pond filled with giant koi fish. I'd sat by that pond many days with Mom, hoping that somehow, she'd find her way back to me.

Harry turned right down another hall, and I followed, realizing we were heading away from the common area.

"She's in her room today?" I asked, sad.

"She is. This morning was a rough one. It's why I called you. She was doing good there for a while, but the storm set her off. Found her standing at the window, screaming about war drums and catapults." He shrugged, at a loss as he always was when Mom went off on one of her tangents. "We sedated her to calm her down. She's awake, but she hasn't said much. I'd hoped her seeing you would help."

I smiled but kept my negative thoughts to myself. Mom seeing me hardly did anything. She didn't recognize me, not since she came back from wherever the hell she'd been for four years. The year I turned twenty-one, she vanished from our home, tucked away in the forests of Oregon. I'd already been back in class and living on campus. By the time I realized she was missing, the cops had no idea how long she'd been gone. I never gave up, and the detective on her case didn't either, but there was no trail to follow. Mom simply disappeared.

Then, one night two months ago, I received a phone call from the detective saying someone matching Mom's description was brought to the local hospital. I'd gone, excited to have her back, only it wasn't her. Physically, she'd come home, but mentally, she was gone. She couldn't answer any questions about where she'd been and kept talking about goblins, of all things. I told Harry and her other doctors I thought she might be somehow referring to the stories she'd told me when I was little. She talked about goblin wars and elves in some far-off fairytale world. How there was a hero destined to save everyone, a brave elf named Garrick. She used to tease how one day I'd meet him and become as courageous as he was.

But I never met an elf named Garrick and had grown up without turning into some brave hero. I was happy with my books and reading about others doing heroic deeds. These mad musings of hers, though, were starting to get to me. Two nights ago, I had a vivid dream of some insane fight between monsters and warriors. There'd been a red-haired man with pointed ears. In the dream, he looked right at me. It was the weirdest thing. I couldn't remember the last time I'd had a dream that clear.

"Nienna? You sure you're up for this today?"

I nodded, keeping the smile planted on my face. "I'm her daughter. I have to be, right?" I reached for the door, but he stopped me. "I'm okay, really."

"You've been through just as much as she has. If you need to come back—"

"No," I insisted, though it wasn't because I was strong. It was because I was weak, and I knew it. If I left now, I wouldn't be able to bring myself to come back tomorrow. "I can see her."

Harry opened the door, and I stepped into the room that had been Mom's residence for the last four months. I'd decorated the walls with a few pictures from home in hopes it'd jar her memory. The doctors had told me anything could trigger them.

"Mom?" I spotted her sitting in the rocking chair by the window. She had her favorite plaid blanket across her lap and wore her dark blue cardigan. Her brown hair was braided and hung over her shoulder. If I didn't know any better, I'd say she was a perfectly sane woman. But she gave no indication she realized I was there. "Mom?" I took her hand and gave it a squeeze. "It's Nienna."

Her light brown eyes, which looked nothing like mine, shifted toward my face. I held my breath, waiting. Her lips parted, but the words she said next had nothing to do with me. "They're coming," she whispered. "The drums. Don't you hear the drums?"

I hid my disappointment behind a sad smile. "No, Mom, there are no drums."

"Yes, there are. I hear them. They're coming for you just as they did for me. They're coming to get you, Nienna."

"No one's—wait, Mom? You just said my name." I glanced at Harry, standing in the doorway. He nodded, his brow furrowed. I didn't imagine it. "Mom, can you hear me?"

She squeezed my hand, and hopeful tears pricked my eyes. "Goblins, Nienna. The goblins are coming to get you. I see them, see them everywhere. Going to get you, going to get you," she repeated until she ran out of air. She sucked in a deep breath, and the cackle that escaped her mouth was dark and eerie.

I tried to pull my hand free, but she held on so tightly, I winced.

Harry rushed over, prying Mom's hand off mine. "Time to relax, Millie," he said as she kept laughing.

I backed away as he helped her out of her chair and tried to guide her to bed. They made it three steps when Mom lost it, and her laughter turned into screams. She kept shoving at Harry, reaching for me, eyes filled with fear. I clapped a hand over my mouth and backed away.

Two orderlies ran in, responding to Harry's shout. Mom's shrieks grew louder.

I had to leave the room. Less than a minute later, it became quiet, and Harry joined me in the hall. He didn't say anything, only rested his hand on my shoulder. I peeked into the room.

Mom was back in bed, asleep already, her body, legs, and arms held down by straps.

"I'm sorry," Harry finally said. "She hasn't had an episode like that in weeks."

"She said my name," I whispered. "You heard that, too, right?"

"I did, but I don't want you getting your hopes up. It's a start, but she has a long way to go before she's fully recovered."

I nodded, knowing he was right, but I couldn't help it. Mom hadn't said my name since she'd been back. "Call me if anything happens."

"I will."

He gave me a quick hug, and I left, my heart torn between wanting to believe Mom was coming back to me and worried it was merely a fluke.

I was meeting Phil for lunch at the café on campus, so I took a cab back across town. When I reached the café, my hair was soaking wet and dripping down my back. Phil was at our usual table in the back corner, his nose buried in a book. I took a second to admire his handsome features accented by the bit of stubble on his cheeks. His brow wrinkled as he turned a page, shoving up his reading glasses as they slipped down his nose.

Phillip Waxon and I had been dating for the last year and a half. We met during our undergrad years, and our love of history brought us together. He dealt more with authentication of historical documents and artifacts, whereas I dealt with the research end studying anything from the Medieval era and prior. He asked me out in the library one night, and that was also where we shared our first kiss. I smiled, thinking of that night in the stacks, but that night seemed so long ago. As the months went on, I knew Phil wasn't the guy I should be with. Or rather, I wasn't the right woman for him. Picking at my nails, I willed myself to have enough courage to tell him the truth. And like every time before, I faltered and told myself I'd do it tomorrow.

"Hey," he said brightly when I joined him at the table. "You know, they have these handy inventions called umbrellas."

"News said it wasn't going to rain today. Besides, I loaned it to a student last week."

He smirked. "You're never going to get it back. What have I told you?"

"I'm too nice. I know, I know," I muttered and was grateful for the cup of coffee already waiting for me. I held the hot mug between my hands and sighed.

Phil closed his book, and then his hands were on mine. "Do you want to talk about it?"

I shook my head, not sure I could make it through a conversation about Mom without completely falling apart. I'd managed not to sob like a maniac in the back of the cab. Making a scene in the café where I knew at least half the patrons didn't sound like a great idea either.

"You sure?"

"Yeah, I mean, it wasn't great," I murmured. "But she said my name. Twice. Said it twice."

"That's good. Why aren't you happier?"

"Because while she was saying my name, she

kept muttering about hearing war drums and goblins coming to get me," I snapped, cringing. "Sorry. I'm sorry."

"You're allowed to be stressed. I can take it."

"You shouldn't have to. I just don't understand. Who would drive someone crazy like this? For what? Entertainment? I still have no idea where she was all those years, or what she went through." A tear slipped from my eye, and hastily, I wiped it away. "She's all I have left of my family, and now I don't even have her. I'm alone."

Phil wrapped his arm around my shoulder. "You're not alone. You've got Alice and me, at least."

Alice was my best friend, had been since freshman year. She would've given me a lecture if I'd said those words to her.

I leaned into Phil's side and told myself I shouldn't be enjoying this. It wasn't fair to either of us. If I was going to be brutally honest with myself, the only thing we really had in common was our love of history. I was holding him back. He wanted to travel the world, explore, go on digs, disappear into the wilds for months at a time. He talked about getting out of Portland all the time. I was the one who went along with his planning, telling myself I'd find an excuse not to go when the time came. I'd hoped by now he would've picked up on the lack of chemistry between us and broken up with me. Sadly, that hadn't happened yet.

"Are you working tonight?" he asked.

"Yeah, two to close."

"Maybe you should take the day off for once. Give yourself a break."

"I can't leave Alice alone. She gets creeped out at night."

"She's an adult, and I think she'd want you to take care of yourself," he said with a laugh. "When is she going to stop believing in ghosts?"

"Who says ghosts aren't real? I believe in them."

"Since when?"

I shrugged, thankful he was particularly good at distracting me from the stress of dealing with Mom. "Since always. Ghosts and things that go bump in the night. There's no proof that they don't exist."

"I think you mean there's no proof they do exist."

"Whatever. You don't have to believe, but I do. It'd be nice to think fairies are out there, cheering people up with their fairy dust, or I don't know. Stop laughing," I said, chuckling and smacking his shoulder. "I might be a historian, but don't you ever wonder if all the old tales are true? They had to come from somewhere."

"Like the stories your mom told you? Goblins and elves? Come on. It's called people's fear and lack of understanding."

I shrugged, watching the rain patter the windows of the café. "You're probably right." I squinted, trying to see through the downpour. For a second, I thought that Alred guy was standing across the street. I blinked, and there was no one there.

We ordered our usual club sandwiches and enjoyed our lunch date. We were both TAs, and he had classes this afternoon. Mine weren't until Friday, something I was extremely grateful for. I wasn't sure I could stand up and give lectures for Professor Gibbins and not fall apart halfway through. A nice quiet afternoon and night in the library always did the trick of soothing my fraying nerves.

At two on the dot, I swiped my badge to clock in for my shift at the library. Alice was fifteen minutes late. Her hair was a mess, and she couldn't stop grinning, skidding across the stone floor and around the circulation desk.

"Where were you?" I asked while she tried to fix her hair.

"Oh, you know, just out and about."

I picked up a stack of books ready to be scanned back in, eyeing Alice over the top of them. "You were with Jeff."

"What? No," she answered in a rush, her cheeks turning bright red.

"I thought we talked about this. He doesn't want a girlfriend."

"Trust me, I know."

"Then why are you doing this to yourself?"

"Because maybe I like having hookups now and again. Make me feel alive. Not all of us can be lucky like you. I have to get my fixes somewhere."

I nodded slowly, feeling her eyes on me.

"Wait, Nienna, please tell me you and Phil—"

"Nope," I replied, cutting her question off. "And can we not talk about that here?"

"Like anyone's listening."

"Still, we can talk about it at home." I loaded the pushcart with books to be returned to their shelves and left her behind the desk, shaking her head and muttering about my being too nice.

The day I met Alice Silvan was certainly one I wouldn't forget. We were freshmen roommates in the dorms. She was around when Mom disappeared, and she'd been there every day since. I never really had a best friend growing up, but I sure as hell had one now. We lived in a small apartment on campus and knew everything about each other. She was a hopeless romantic, always searching for that one guy to sweep her off her feet. She talked about how jealous she was that I found Phil all the time. I'd put on a smile and act like she was right.

I wanted her to be right. I wanted one thing in my life to be easy. Phil was a great guy. I should be ecstatic that I got him all to myself, but something was missing. It was true we hadn't gone too far past some heated making out sessions. I was the one holding us back in that regard, too.

I headed to the east wing, which most students avoided because, like Alice, they thought it was creepy. I didn't mind the dim lighting or the lack of windows. I pushed the cart to the very back room, noting the books that needed to be put up here, not surprised to find myself completely alone. The collections in this wing were incredibly old and hardly ever checked out. Six rows of shelves were placed toward the back of the room, and four in the front with four long, narrow tables set up in the very center of the area. Lamps sat in the middle of the wooden tabletops to give the reader more light. A couple had been left on, and I went to turn them off. As I hummed quietly to myself, taking my time and enjoying the peace and quiet, my thoughts drifted from what to do about Phil to that guy I met yesterday.

Alred.

It wasn't a name I'd heard before. Then again, neither was mine. I smiled, recalling the details of his costume and his mannerisms as if he'd stepped right out of medieval times. His bright, green eyes had stood out from his tanned face. He'd smiled, but his eyes were hard, almost cold. The gold flecks in them made me curious, remembering how they'd shimmered in the sunlight. His black beard gave him a rugged, handsome vibe, along with the long, jagged scar on his neck. That hadn't looked fake. I wondered what would give someone a scar like that. Car accident, maybe?

Putting another book on the shelf, I shook my head at how my imagination was running away from me. The clothes he'd worn had highlighted the broadness of his shoulders and how muscled he was. His dark brown coat had hung to his knees, patches sewn on here and there from wear and tear. The hood had hung low and had what I thought was some sort of cowl with it. His black leather pants and knee-high boots were just as worn as the rest of his clothing; bits of mud were caked on them as if he'd trekked across miles by foot. Those bracers on his forearms had been the best bit, along with the black shirt he wore beneath his coat. Every bit of what he wore appeared authentic, and damn, did he look fine in all of it.

I bit my lip, closing my eyes for just a moment.

Phil was handsome, but he was lean. There was hardly any muscle to him. But that Alred, he was all man. I sighed, giving my head a shake. "Now you sound like Alice. Stop daydreaming like you're a horny teenager. So, he was sexy as hell in that leather. Doesn't matter. He probably wants adventure, just like Phil does, which means you're out of luck."

My face grew warm, picturing Alred's face and the rest of him. I went to place another book on the shelf and missed. It fell to the floor.

I cursed, bending to pick it up and straightened, yelping in surprise at the pair of green eyes with gold flecks staring at me from the other side of the bookshelf.

"Alred? Shit," I muttered through a laugh. "Scared me."

His brow furrowed, and he scratched at his beard. "Thought I told you to watch your surroundings."

I shook my head, glancing around. "I'm in the library. Not like I have much to watch." I placed the book on the shelf, listening to his heavy steps as he came around and joined me. He wore the same getup from yesterday. His jaw clenched, and his eyes narrowed. For a brief second, I wondered if I should yell for security. His gaze latched onto mine a second later, and the weirdest sense that I would always be safe with him shot through my mind. Yeah, today was definitely a weird one.

I reached my hand out, not sure what I was planning on doing. His gaze shifted to it, and I let it fall.

"Sorry, I'm having an off day," I mumbled. "What are you doing here? Following me?" I teased.

"Negative," he replied. "That would be odd."

I blinked a few times, noting the forced smile on his face. "Uh-huh. It would be odd. So, uh, what are you doing here?"

"Finishing our conversation."

"Right. I honestly don't even remember what we were talking about." I pushed the cart along.

Alred followed, his hands clasped behind his ramrod-straight back.

"You in the military or something?"

"I was trained as a fighter from a young age, yes, but I'm not in the military."

More questions flooded my mind as we strolled along, with me putting books on the shelves and Alred looking as if he was suddenly my bodyguard. "What is it you do then? Oh, wait, is this all part of the fair stuff? You're really committed, staying in character like this."

"I'm not part of this fair you keep mentioning."

"No? Then you just wear all this for fun?"

"It's who I am," he answered. "There's much to tell you, but I sense you'll need proof if you're to believe anything I say."

"Did someone put you up to this?" I looked around, expecting to see Alice or Phil hiding behind the shelves, laughing at whatever joke they were playing on me. "I get it, Phil's trying to give me a distraction or something. Convince me to go on an adventure with him. He's out of luck."

As much as I loved Phil and Alice, they were always giving me a hard time about being such a bookworm and a homebody. Always wanting me to just pick up and go on a road trip somewhere or fly to another country. No matter how many times they asked, I told them it'd never happen. I knew of a few companies that hired actors to take people on fake mystical adventures. I'd heard about them and was suddenly annoyed if Phil had paid this actor to bug me. Today wasn't the day for this shit, something he should've realized after speaking to me at lunch.

"Phil has nothing to do with why I'm here," Alred muttered, practically growling out the man's name. "This is no joke and no trick. I need you to understand who you truly are, Nienna."

The smile I'd been wearing to play along fell at his serious tone. "What are you talking about?"

He crossed his left arm over his chest and bowed. "I am Alred Lightvale of the Fourleaf Court in the land of Kenzu'grote. I am charged with the duty of protecting the Goblin Historian with my life. You are the new Historian, Nienna Havard, and it's time you embrace your true calling." He straightened.

I couldn't help it. I burst out laughing. "That was good, really good." I barely managed to get the words out between guffaws.

He rolled his eyes toward the ceiling, reaching for his right hip. He removed a leather pouch and stuck his hand inside. He muttered quietly, but the words were foreign to me. French? No, something else, something soothing to my ears that tugged at a distant memory of another man speaking similar words. I wanted to ask him what he was saying when he removed a small book that fit in the size of his palm.

"What is that?" I asked, panicking.

He took my hand, placed the book on it. Immediately, my palm warmed, and a burst of air blew my hair back. He tapped the cover and stepped away. "Your destiny."

As soon as he removed his hand, the book grew. I was left gape-mouthed, the weight increasing, and I had to use both hands to keep it from falling. When it finally stopped expanding, a massive leather-bound tome with a black cover was in my hands. Intricate designs were etched into it, curling and twisting in a maddening storm of vines and small flowers. There was no title on the spine, but words glimmered in gold on the cover in a language I couldn't read.

"What... how... how did you do that?" I stammered.

"Magic. Take this and read it. Inside you'll find proof of my words. This world is not where you belong. It has never been. I'll return tomorrow evening to this room at six." He rested his hand on the cover.

I raised my head to find his eyes fixed on mine.

"Read it, Nienna, all of it." He turned sharply and exited the room.

I watched the doorway he left through, waiting for him to come back, laugh, and say this was all a practical joke. But he didn't, and the tome grew even more cumbersome. What the hell was this? And who was he? Unsure of what to do with the information he'd dumped on me, I carefully set the book on the bottom of the cart and went back to work, pretending it hadn't happened. But each time I glanced at the bottom of the cart, the tome was still there. I played over his words repeatedly, waiting for something to click. All it did was give me a headache.

By the time Alice and I were closing the library at eleven, I was bouncing on my feet and picking my nails, wanting to get home so I could look through what Alred left me.

"What's got you all anxious?" Alice asked as we walked across campus toward our apartment.

"Did you see a guy dressed in leather leave the

library?" I asked. Maybe I hallucinated him. Yeah, that was it. I was going crazy, like Mom had.

"I did. It seemed kind of weird, but he walked out fast. Why? And what are you lugging home?" She peered at the cover of the tome. "I don't remember seeing this. What language is that?"

"Not sure. And that guy lent it to me for a new study," I lied. "He's from out of town."

Alice's confused expression said she didn't believe me, but she let it go. Once we reached our apartment, I was about to disappear into my room for the night when Alice called me back.

"We going to talk about Phil?"

"Nope. I'm going to bed."

"Oh, come on," she complained. "Something's bugging you and don't lie. You suck at it."

I tried not to laugh. "Really?"

"Fine, you don't, but you've been acting off for a while now when it comes to Phil. You two doing okay?"

I puffed out my cheeks, not sure how much I should admit to Alice. She didn't exactly understand the meaning of keeping things to herself. "He thinks we are, but no." I shrugged. "Not that he's done anything wrong," I added quickly. "But I feel like we're not getting anywhere, and it's my fault."

"What do you mean?"

"The more I'm around him, the more I realize I'm not his type." I sank onto the couch. "He keeps talking about going to all these amazing places and making plans, and I keep going along with them all because I'm an idiot. I don't want to leave Portland. I don't want to go on digs, but I keep agreeing with what he wants."

Alice crossed her arms, sighing. "How many times have I told you? You're too nice. If you don't want to go on these trips, then tell him."

"I try, but then words simply won't come out of my mouth. Plus, he gets so excited about those trips." I held my head in my hands, mumbling, "I need to break up with him, but I'm too much of a freaking chicken to do it."

"Better to do it now than to keep stringing him along." She sat on the couch beside me, nudging me with her elbow. "It'll suck, but it'll be better for you both. And now, you get to be my wingman—erm, woman," she said with a wink.

"Great, that's exactly what I want to do."

"What? It'll be fun to have you back out there with me, braving the dating world together. Break up with Phil, and then you and I can have a fun girls' night out. We'll go bar hopping."

I wanted to say no, but just like with Phil, I couldn't say no to Alice's grinning face. "Yeah, sounds like a great time."

She hugged me, and I squeezed her back. I smiled and stood, telling her I was going to bed. I dragged the massive tome with me into my room, shut the door, and dumped it on my desk. I went about my nightly routine, put on my comfy yoga pants and a hoodie, and finally sat down at the desk. At least I had something to distract me from my Phil and Alice issues.

"It's just a book," I told myself, reaching a shaking hand toward the cover. "What could possibly go wrong from reading it?"

I flipped open the cover, and a hot gust of wind had me hopping out of my chair and whirling around. The sharp smell of something burning hit my nose, and I sneezed.

"Okay, weird, that was weird." I steadied my nerves and forced myself back to the desk. The first page was blank, and I turned it, noting the rough texture of the paper. It was thick, and my fingers tingled the longer I held it. Telling myself this was all crazy, and I was, in fact, losing it, I glanced at the second page.

I read out loud, "*The Goblin Chronicles of Kenzu'*-

grote, Years 1892-2019, Recorded by Historian Garrick Havard of the Fourleaf Court." I paused. "Wait. What?"

Havard. Garrick Havard.

Havard.

My last name. That was my last name written on that page, but the first name had my stomach twisting in knots. The name of Mom's elven hero from the stories. Why was it in this book with my last name? Running a hand down my face, I told myself to shut the book and shove it aside. Instead, I found myself flipping to the next page and was sucked into every single word I read.

—————————————————

Chapter 3
ALRED

—————————————————

At six in the evening, I checked the doorway, but Nienna wasn't here. Grunting in annoyance, I stalked back the other direction, rolling my right shoulder. My wound was healing, slowly, but it throbbed, and my shoulder resisted too much movement.

I hadn't planned on being in the human world this long. With Garrick gone, I needed to report to the Council with the new Historian. No Protector before me ever had to go through this much hassle.

Nienna was the first half-elf Historian since the beginning of Kenzu'grote. It wasn't hard to understand why.

As I waited, I glanced over the shelves filled with books. She had seemed at peace in this dank room though I wasn't sure why. It was musty, and there were no windows and only one door. This was the perfect location to become trapped in and killed.

There was no way to know if the goblins had entered the human world yet. With any luck, they were still seeking out the Historian back home. Either way, I was running out of time. The longer it took for Nienna to accept her calling, the more chances of both worlds falling into chaos. Garrick had started the work of regaining balance, but Nienna needed to finish what he could not.

Footsteps rushed down the narrow hall toward the room. I pressed my back flat to the wall, my hand slipping to the dagger at my hip. Using the shelves to keep me hidden from sight, I waited.

"Alred?" Nienna called.

I revealed myself.

She jumped, glaring at me. "Do you have to keep doing that?"

"Doing what?"

"Giving me a freaking heart attack. And this," she snapped, dropping the tome on a table with a loud thud, "what is this?"

"Did you not read it?"

"I did," she muttered. "I read every single damned page."

Noting the bags under her eyes, I believed her. "Then I'm not sure what you're asking. If you read it, then you should know exactly what it is."

"Seriously?" She raised her hands, miming strangling me. "Why is my last name in it?"

"That doesn't matter. What does is that you're the next Goblin Historian."

Nienna gave me a blank stare, shook her head, and backed away. "That name, Garrick, why is it in a book about goblin wars? This is a fairy tale, right? Some old book about some make-believe world. It has to be. Goblins don't exist. Nothing that's in that book can be real. They're just stories. It has to be where she got them from."

I didn't follow some of what she said and decided to answer the question I could. "Not a fairy tale. It's real, all of it is real."

She sputtered, her eyes wide, and she picked frantically at her nails. "Look, I don't know what kind of sick joke you're trying to play here, but I'm finished. Take your damned book back and leave me alone."

She shoved the tome across the table and started to leave. I caught her wrist, and she opened her mouth. "If you scream, I'll knock you over the head," I warned.

Her mouth clamped shut, but she didn't look afraid. Instead, she looked pissed off. With the way she was rambling, I expected her to fall apart and lose it, not get angry. Maybe she had more of Garrick in her than I first realized.

"I have come a long way to ensure you receive this tome and learn the truth of who you are. I cannot leave the human world for my home until you agree to come with me."

"Nothing coming out of your mouth right now is making any sense."

"It would if you truly read the book."

"I did read it," she snapped, trying to yank her wrist free. My grip was like iron, and she gave up with an exasperated yell. "You want me to simply accept that everything I read last night, those goblin wars, the battles, the new powers rising and falling, the elves…" She trailed off, hanging her head. "I can't believe I'm talking like this. I sound like Mom."

"Millie," I said without thinking.

She twisted her hand in my shirt as if she was strong enough to threaten me. "How do you know her name? How? Who are you?"

"I've told you who I am," I replied calmly, glancing at her hand. "Nienna, you need to take a deep breath and calm yourself."

"Why?"

"Because there's no time for you to have a mental breakdown. I am Alred Lightvale, sworn Protector of the Historian. I have come to find you and bring you back to Kenzu'grote. I cannot leave until you do so. If you come with me, everything will be explained. I swear to you upon my life, no harm shall befall you."

She released me and stepped back, but there was no more panic in her eyes. Her gaze had turned curious, and she laughed nervously. "You sound sincere."

"Because I am. This is my calling, to protect you, just as I did the previous Historian."

"The previous Historian," she repeated. "Garrick Havard."

I nodded, watching her carefully when she backed away but didn't run for the door.

"Why does he have my last name, Alred? I grew up on stories about his being some great hero for the elves. It's what Mom told me before I went to sleep every night. You're saying he's real. Why do we share a name?"

"Does this mean you believe me then?"

She sank into a chair suddenly, her face paling. "How am I supposed to simply believe anything you're saying to me?"

"I'm afraid you don't have a choice."

"Actually, I do. Now tell me, who is Garrick Havard?"

I hesitated, and she slammed her palm on the table.

"I swear if you don't tell me right now, I'm walking out that door, and if you try to follow me, I'll start screaming and have you arrested."

I didn't tell her no human would be able to arrest me. I let it go. "Garrick Havard was your father."

Her face paled even more, and I braced myself to rush forward and catch her if she fainted.

"I'm sorry, could you say that again?"

"Your father was not of the human world. He was an elf."

Her lips twitched, and she laughed again, but the sound was far from happy. "Wow, okay, yeah, I'm just going to go now."

"You can't."

"Yeah, I can."

"No," I snapped and rushed over to prevent her

from leaving. "You are the next Historian. I don't think you understand how serious this situation is. How much danger your life is in."

"I thought you swore to keep me safe?"

"I'm not the one threatening your life. The goblins are. They seek out the next Historian, which is why it's not safe for us to remain here any longer. You have to come with me now."

She held up her hand, and I fell silent. She gulped, shaking her head, and running her hands madly through her messy hair.

"My father was an elf." Her brow wrinkled. "You're talking about him the past tense. He's—is he dead?"

Heart heavy with grief and guilt, I nodded. "I wouldn't be here otherwise. He was killed only a few nights back if we're speaking in human days."

A strange look passed over her face like somehow she knew what night I was talking about. But then she pressed her hands to her face. "Let me get this straight. So, my dad, he was an elf, and he was this Historian or whatever person. And he lived in some other world where you were his protector person? But now you're here to find me because what, you failed your job and he got killed by goblins? Am I following along so far?" She threw her head back, whispering, "I can't believe that all just came out of my mouth. Everything Mom said to me all these years. It doesn't make sense. She was telling the truth? A nightmare, that's all this is. Just one long nightmare."

"It's a lot to take in for someone like you," I agreed. "And there will be time to have all your questions answered, just not right now and not here."

"No."

My brow arched. "No? What do you mean, no?"

"I mean, I'm not doing this." She pushed back from the table, her glare fierce. "I let everyone else push me into doing things I don't want to do, but this, this is too damned much. You don't get to show up here out of nowhere and talk about my dad. I don't know him. I don't know anything about him. Shit, I didn't even know his name. For all I know, you're lying."

"Garrick Havard was a great elf and a great Historian. The work he did for his people," I tried to say, but her hand connected with my face in a slap that left my cheek stinging. Nostrils flaring, I opened my mouth to warn her against such foolishness, and she did it a second time.

"Don't," she whispered, her face screwed up in anger. "Don't you dare tell me that he was a great man or elf or whatever he was. He left us. That's all I know about him. He got my mom pregnant, and then he left us alone. For years. A great man doesn't do that to the people he loves. He doesn't do that to his family."

"The situation was complicated."

She barked a laugh, and her hand balled into a fist. I waited to be punched. Instead, she backed away. Her eyes zeroed in on my cheek, and she held up her hand as if unsure she'd actually hit me. At least I was wrong about Nienna not having any fight in her. It was there, simply buried very, very deep.

"Don't tell me about complicated. And you, you said my mom's name, which means you know her, don't you?"

A rush of regret I hadn't felt in a long while settled on my shoulders. "I do."

I sensed Nienna's mind racing, and she backed away, realization coming over her making her pale once again. "You know what happened to her, why she's crazy."

"It was a terrible accident. Your father and I did all we could to get her back home safely."

"She isn't safe! She's lost her mind," Nienna shouted. "No, you know what? I don't believe you. I don't believe any of this shit. I can't."

"Nienna," I tried, but she backed away even further.

"Stay away from me, got it? I won't let you make me go insane, too."

I quickly reached for the tome, and after tapping it on the cover, shrunk it down once again. "At least take this with you," I urged, following her. "Please. You might not believe me yet, but the truth will find its way to you, and when it does, you need to be ready."

She hesitated, snatched the book out of my hands, left me with one more withering glare, and strode quickly away from me.

I bashed my fist into the nearest wall, putting it easily through the wood paneling. No one was around to see, thankfully. I kicked the bit of debris to the side and exited the library. My plan was to keep tabs on Nienna. That conversation had not gone as I planned, and I was worried about what she might do with the information I gave her. Knocking her over the head and dragging her back to Kenzu'grote seemed like a much better plan. And simpler.

I exited the library, using the compass to track Nienna's movements. There was no head of reddish-blond hair on the sidewalk, and I took off in the direction she headed. If she couldn't come to terms with the truth by tomorrow night, she'd leave me no choice but to drag her kicking and screaming to where she belonged.

I shouldn't have said her mother's name or mentioned Garrick. That seemed to have set her off. As guilty as I felt over leaving Garrick to his fate, what Millie went through should never have happened. Her current state of insanity rested solely on me, no matter what Garrick had tried to tell me. I was the one who told him bringing Millie to Kenzu'grote wouldn't end well, but he insisted. If I'd fought harder against his wishes, Millie might not be in the state she was in. Once Nienna was old enough to be on her own, Garrick and I had returned to the human world to retrieve Millie. Finally, they could be together without fear of a child being involved. For Millie, it had been twenty-five years of living without the person she loved, but for Garrick, it had been fifty. Time passed differently in our world.

I'd watched over them both while we traveled through the kingdoms. A part of me grew jealous at seeing how happy they were and how in love. But I wasn't the only one watching. Goblins raided our camp one night and stole Millie away, holding her captive for months. By the time we rescued her, it was too late.

The compass continued to point me on until a panicked shout, coming from the copse of trees, drew my attention. The campus was mostly empty at this time in the evening, and I sprinted, unsure of what I'd find, but at least there were no witnesses.

I drew my dagger, coming across the small clearing and the body lying in the center of it. His throat had been ripped out. Dead eyes stared at me in shock. The tracks surrounding the body were all too familiar.

Goblins.

They were here already.

Nienna was in far more danger than I first believed.

She was out of time.

We both were.

Chapter 4
NIENNA

Lugging that damned tome across campus with me the next morning, I stifled another yawn. Too bad, I couldn't figure out how to shrink the freaking thing down to a nice tiny size. After I argued with Alred, I searched through the tome again, willing what I saw to make sense. All it did was leave me feeling positive I was indeed losing my mind. My only saving grace was Alice had seen Alred, too. He, at least, was real.

It was everything else I was calling into question.

I replayed Mom's stories over and over in my head, along with everything she'd said since coming home. Events that took place in the early years of the tome lined up with what she'd talked about when I was little. Great battles waged over territory. Mighty elvish knights fighting against goblin clans. With every word, another piece of the story fell into place. And all the while, in the back of my mind, I heard Alred telling me Garrick was my father. I hadn't slept at all last night. Finally, I left my bedroom with a pounding headache, a churning stomach, and the thought that my life was about to be turned completely inside out.

I entered the building where Phil spent most of his spare time researching and authenticating artifacts brought in by the university. It didn't take me long to track him down, and I dropped my tote bag with the tome on his workstation.

"Nienna? You look terrible, are you alright?"

"No. I'm not alright," I replied. "Rough night."

"Alice said you locked yourself in your room when you came home. I tried calling you," Phil said, reaching for my hand. "Talk to me. What's going on? This about your mom?"

I was worried the second I opened my mouth, the only thing that would come out was mad laughter. Thunder rumbled loudly outside with the approaching storm making me jump. Phil gave me a concerned look that I waved away. "No, it's not about her. I uh, I need you to do me a favor."

"Okay," he said slowly. "What is it?"

I tugged the tome out of my bag, resting my hand on the cover. Absently, my fingers traced the grooves and dents of the embossed vines. "I need you to see if this is authentic and how old."

"Where did you find that?"

"Someone left it in the library," I lied. I was doing a lot of that lately. Grinding my teeth, I told myself it was for a good reason. I pushed the tome toward Phil. "Can you do it?"

"Yeah, of course, I can."

"I mean, like right now."

He pulled the tome toward him, tapping his fingers on the cover. "It shouldn't be an issue. I don't have much work today. You sure you're alright?"

"I'm great."

His brow rose, and he took my hands. "No, you're not. You've got bags under your eyes, and you look a mess. You never look a mess. Talk to me, please. That's all I'm asking here."

I bit the inside of my cheek. Here it was, the chance for me to end it with Phil so I could stop feeling so guilty every time I was with him. The words were on my lips, but I clamped my mouth shut at the last second. I mentally yelled at myself to stop being a coward when a flash of lightning lit up the room. The rumbling thunder that followed shook the walls. The power flickered for a second. Rain battered the windows, and Phil looked away from me. I sighed in relief, tugging my hands back.

"Nienna?"

"We'll talk, soon, I promise," I said, backing away.

"Wait. Is this about us? Are we okay?"

I winced without meaning to, and he reached for me again. I stayed out of his grasp, holding up my hands. "I–I'm sorry. I can't do this right now."

"Did I do something wrong?"

"What? No, you did nothing wrong, Phil, nothing. This is all on me."

Sadness filled his eyes, along with confusion, and there it was. Hurt.

I hung my head, wishing I kept my mouth shut. "Look, you have to have figured out by now I'm not the woman you think I am. You need someone who's, well, not me. Someone willing to follow through with all these trips of yours and go on adventures. I can't do that, and I'm sorry I let you think I even wanted to." Yeah, I was making total sense. "I swear we'll talk later about everything, but I need you to know you're a great guy. You are."

"Just not for you," he said quietly. He cleared his throat roughly and avoided my eyes. "I'll uh, I'll run some tests on this for you. Should have the results by tonight."

"Thanks, Phil. I owe you one."

"No, it's fine. Just helping my—my friend."

My heart sank at his words, but he wasn't the only person I needed to see today. I thought about hugging him to cheer him up, but that'd make everything worse. I hurried out of the lab, not wanting to go back on what I'd just said. Phil deserved to have a girlfriend who wasn't going to hold him back from chasing his dreams. Who wanted to explore the world at his side. He'd see that in time, I hoped. This was not how I wanted to break up with him, but too late to take any of it back now.

By the time I reached the institution housing Mom, the storm had grown even more furious. I was drenched simply by running from the cab to the front doors. No sane person would be out in this weather, but I had to talk to Mom. If everything Alred told me was true, which was a huge if, then what Mom had been ranting about had to be as well. I met Harry at the front desk, and he gave me a concerned glance.

"Nienna? What's going on?"

"I need to see her," I told him. "Please. I just, I need to talk to her."

"She hasn't said a word since your last visit. Are you sure?"

"I don't have a choice."

He sucked in a breath at my words and pulled me to the side of the lobby. "Are you alright?"

"No, I'm not," I snapped, hanging my head at my tone. "I'm sorry. Someone I met recently said some things, and I need to see if they're true. He knew Mom and—please, Harry? Five minutes, that's all I'm asking."

"Five minutes," he agreed, and I was buzzed into the main facility.

At Mom's door, he opened it, stepped back, and I ran inside to find her in the rocking chair, blanket on her lap, watching the storm.

"I haven't seen a storm like this in years," Harry muttered while the power flickered. "All she wants to do is watch it, though." He glanced at his watch. "Five minutes."

"Thanks, Harry."

He went back to the hall, giving me time alone with Mom. She made no indication she saw me at all. I moved until I stood right in front of her, willing her gaze to focus on me. Lightning flashed around the room, and her eyes narrowed. I held my breath, waiting, but she relaxed and stayed focused on the storm.

"Mom?" I rested my hand on hers, giving it a squeeze. "Everything you've been saying since you've been back, is it real?" I whispered, not believing what I was saying. "The goblins and the war, you're telling the truth, aren't you? Those stories. They were never merely stories." I licked my lips, crouching in front of her. "Alred Lightvale, he came to me and started telling me all this crazy shit about Dad and you and goblins. But it can't be real. None of it can be. Another world, filled with elves and goblins?"

Mom fidgeted in her chair but said nothing.

"He told me about Dad," I went on. "Says he was Garrick. The hero in those tales. I don't understand any of this. Why wouldn't you tell me the truth? That he was an elf and a Historian? I guess it does sound too crazy to be real, but I don't know what to think right now. I'm so confused." I took both her hands. "Please, I need to know what's real and what's not. He said Dad's dead and I have to go with him now. Then there's this book and——"

Her hand slipped free of mine and cupped my

cheek. I glanced up to find her eyes clear and looking at me. A sad frown wrinkled her brow.

"Your father's dead?"

"Mom?"

She nodded. "I'm sorry, hon, so sorry for every-thing." She moved her other hand to my face. "Garrick. I loved that elf, and now he's gone." Tears shimmered in her eyes, but her shoulders tensed, then she gave herself a firm nod. "If he's dead and Alred is here, then your time has come. I'm sorry, Nienna. I'm so sorry I wasn't able to tell you anything sooner."

I waited for her to slip away from me again, but her eyes remained clear.

My heart sank. "So, it's true? All of it?"

"Our greatest fear for you has come true. I hoped he was wrong, but the tome never is," she murmured, kissing my forehead. "You have a great destiny awaiting you, sweetheart. You can't turn your back on it now."

I shut my eyes, tears falling down my cheeks. "I don't want a great destiny. I only want you to be better. I want you to come back to me. I can't just up and leave."

"There's far more to you than you realize," she assured me. "You can do this. You're strong."

"No, I'm not. Please, Mom, tell me this is all a joke. I need you to come back to me. That's all I want."

"I know, but the madness, it's clouding my mind." Her words shook with fear. She took hold of my hands, and I stared into those eyes already beginning to glaze over again. "Trust him, Nienna, you must trust Alred. He is your Protector. It won't be long before they find you. You can't let them take you, understand me? You can't. I won't have you end up like me."

"What are you talking about? Who?"

"The goblins. They seek the Historian. They seek to change the tides of war. You must go with Alred. There is no other path. The fate of everyone is on you now, sweetheart. I'm sorry." She smiled sadly. "You have your father's eyes and his spirit. Don't forget who you are. Don't forget…" Her words trailed off, her gaze taking on a faraway look. "War drums. Don't you hear the war drums?"

"Mom?"

She muttered incoherently.

Harry joined me and gently pulled me away, telling me she needed her rest now.

I gave Mom one last worried look and ran out

of her room. Harry called after me, but I had to get away from there.

"Alice?" I yelled when I reached our apartment a half-hour later. "You home?"

There was no answer.

I tossed my tote bag on the couch, stomping around the living room. Nothing made sense. Nothing. Mom had said to trust Alred, but how? How the hell was I supposed to trust a guy who showed up out of nowhere and told me that my dad, who I've never met, was dead? And, oh yeah, by the way, you're some Goblin Historian? Who was Mom kidding? I was nothing like the hero in those tales. I didn't want to go on some grand adventure and fight goblins. I didn't want to save kingdoms and go to some magical land no one had ever heard of. I wasn't like Garrick.

I was simply Nienna. The bookworm who was happiest in the library, alone, with nothing but pages and pages of history to keep me company. I didn't do anything heroic, and I sure as hell didn't go looking for fights.

"You're losing it," I muttered to myself. "That's all this is. You're finally hitting your breaking point. That's it. Finished."

I sank onto the couch and scowled at the floor.

Goblins and elves. I laughed madly at the idea that they were real, then laughed louder when I remembered arguing with Phil over whether fantastical creatures existed or not. I'd said they did, and here I was, faced with that truth, and I couldn't get myself to accept what stared me in the face.

Unless the tome I gave to Phil ended up being fake.

Scrambling off the couch, I rushed to grab my phone, digging frantically through my tote until I found it. There were already several missed calls from Phil. The first message was from him, apologizing for pushing me and wanting to make sure we were going to talk later. He wasn't ready to give up on us. I knew breaking up with him wasn't going to be that easy. Right now, with the way my life was turning into a sloppy mess, the best place for him was far away from me. The second message he asked why my last name was in the book.

"This is weird," his message went on. "These pages, they're nothing like I've seen before. And this leather? It's not fake, but it's not from any identifiable animal. I'm going to have to keep running tests, but Nienna, whatever this thing is, I think it's authentic. Just call me back when you can. I'll be at the lab for the rest of the day.

There's something strange about these dates, too. Everything that happens in this book coincides with something terrible. Natural disasters mostly. I don't know what this is, but I'm going to figure this out."

My phone slipped from my hand, clattering to the floor. The tome was real, which meant everything Alred and Mom said, was that real, too? If Dad was an elf, that made me part elf. I fumbled with the gold bracelet on my wrist, shaking my head and pacing from one end of the living room to the other. It was on my fifth pass by the coffee table I noticed it.

"Where did you come from?"

Sitting in the center of the table was a small wood carving of a wolf. Its head was thrown back in a howl, and it had a red symbol etched into its side. I picked it up, unsure of where it came from. Alice didn't buy stuff like this. Curious, I ran my hands over the rough angles and laid it in my palm.

With a sharp crack of lightning, it hit me, and a shiver of pure fear slipped down my spine. "Red Wolf Clan," I whispered, recalling one of the names of the Goblin clans.

I dropped the wolf to the floor, backing away. I had to get out of here. I had to run.

The floorboards creaked, coming from my bedroom.

I froze. I hadn't turned on any lights when I arrived, and the apartment was dark from the raging storm outside. It didn't stop me from seeing the hulking shadow in the doorway to my bedroom.

Another creak to my right.

I whipped my head around.

A second shadow, this one in Alice's doorway.

Lightning flashed, giving me a brief glimpse of who or what stood in my apartment.

Their massive size alone shocked me and had my panicked scream dying in my throat. They weren't human. I wasn't even sure how they fit in the doorways with their bulk.

Another flash of lightning.

I noted their skin was dark and weathered, almost maroon in color, and the clothes they wore were ragged bits of cloth and leather. One of them had a few pieces of chainmail, but little else. They had jagged edged swords at their hips, which they drew, stepping into the living room, blocking me in. I gulped, shaking in terror, forced to move to the back door that led to a balcony and a long drop down.

I was trapped.

"Historian," the one on the right snapped, his voice rough on my ears, "you come with us."

"I uh, I don't think I will."

He cackled a high-pitched sound that didn't match his body. "You have nowhere to run." He brandished his sword, already stained red, and reached his other hand toward me. Long, black claws were in the place of fingernails.

I staggered away until my back hit the glass door.

"If you fight, it will only make it worse."

My mouth worked, but nothing came out.

The one on the left had closed in, too. Lightning flashed, giving me a glimpse of their faces, and I took in their narrow, black eyes, and their sharp-angled cheekbones and jaws. They were bald, but their heads were covered in tattoos, as were their cheeks and chins. One of them had bones jutting through his earlobes.

I pinched my arm, willing this to be a nightmare, but they didn't disappear, and I didn't wake up.

"No," I heard myself say.

The creatures I could only assume were goblins cackled again. "Pain is the path you've chosen then.

Suits us fine." He grinned, revealing a mouth full of sharpened teeth.

The one on the right raised his sword.

I turned my head away, bracing for the hit.

The front door burst open.

The goblins whipped around.

I peered between their bodies.

A hooded figure in a familiar leather coat. The hood was thrown back. Alred's eyes narrowed in hate at the goblins. He drew a sword from his back and a dagger from his hip, his brow arching.

"Who gets to die first?" He charged into the room.

Chapter 5
ALRED

After finding the dead student in the clearing on campus, I spent the rest of the evening and, throughout the night, hunting down the goblins responsible. The four I came across had made camp in the woods off-campus. I'd taken them out without gaining any new injuries, but my shoulder didn't appreciate being used to such extent yet. I left the last goblin alive long enough to give me the answers I sought. The ones I killed last night had been half the size of the two who stared me down now.

No matter. They wouldn't be walking out of this apartment with their lives.

The two goblins growled viciously, turning their attention to me. My lip twitched in disgust at the sight of the tattoos marring their faces. They were Loq and Lyz, commanders from the Red Wolf clan.

"Alred," Loq snarled from my right, while his brother cackled. "Appears you're failing. Again."

"Not yet," I muttered.

There was no time to tell Nienna to run. There was nowhere for her to escape to, anyhow. As the goblins made their move, I rushed Loq, sliding in low with my sword. I slashed at his side and stabbed him in the thigh with my dagger. He roared, swinging his jagged blade toward me.

I hit the ground in a roll, cursing the confines of the small living space. Loq was right behind me. Luckily, his blade crashed into the wall and became embedded there. He worked at jerking it free. I kicked him in the chest, sending him stumbling into the kitchen table.

Lyz shouted, then threw me into the wall, bashing my head. He slammed the hilt of his sword toward my face. I slid to the right and stabbed up and under his ribs. His eyes bulged. He gasped as my blade punctured his lung. I withdrew it and stabbed him a second time. That should end his miserable existence.

Black blood coating my hand, I pushed a rapidly weakening Lyz away in time to find Loq yanking his blade free of the wall. At the sight of his wounded brother, he threw back his head with a ferocious bellow. His sword arced over his head and met my blade with a loud clang. I blocked his jabs and stabs, shoving him back across the apartment. He might have been twice my size, but my sword moved too fast for him to keep up.

I hadn't been able to save Garrick from his deadly fate, but I was not about to lose his daughter. He struggled to keep up with my attacks, to no avail. I ran him through with my sword. He grunted, reaching up to grab the blade and yank it free when I slashed my dagger across his throat. Black blood sprayed my front and everything around us as he fell to his knees. He growled to me in goblin, cursing me.

I tore my sword free. His body toppled to the side. I kicked him to ensure he was dead. Wiping my sword and dagger on the sleeve of my overcoat, I sheathed them both and spun around.

"We need to leave," I told Nienna, holding out my hand.

Her mouth hung open, and her eyes were wide. She raised her hand, pointing to Lyz's dead body. "They," she started, stopped, and gulped. "What the hell are they?"

"Goblins. What did you think?" I went to her, took her hand, and dragged her with me through the living room. "We don't have much time. These aren't the only goblins they sent after you."

She followed me then suddenly tore her hand away. "No, just stop."

"We don't have time for this. You can fall apart later." I tried to grab her hand, but she backed away, tripped over Lyz's feet, and fell right into a pool of his sticky black blood.

I waited for a scream, but all she did was curse and sputter, slipping and sliding as she attempted to get up. I took her by her arms and hauled her to her feet.

"Nienna, look at me. Nienna," I snapped, and her wild gaze flicked to mine. "Your life is in danger. You need to come with me right now. I can keep you safe, but not in this world."

I sensed her mind racing as she reached up and squeezed my arms. "It's true then," she whispered. "What I read, what Mom told me, everything about Garrick, it's all true."

"I will tell you everything once you are safe."

"But the goblins... Mom—won't they go after her?"

"No. She's not the Historian. You are. You're

the one they will come after, and it's you I've sworn to protect." I glanced at her blood-soaked clothes and scowled. "I'll grab you fresh clothes. And the tome. We need it."

She cringed, biting her lip. "About that," she muttered.

"Yes?" I asked. I realized what her guilty look must mean. "Nienna, what did you do with the tome?"

"Don't look at me like that," she snapped, her green eyes flaring with annoyance. "I wasn't sure if you were telling the truth, or Mom, so I took the book to Phil to have him test it for me."

"You had him run tests on the tome? Do you have any idea what you've done?"

"No, but guess what? It worked. The book's authentic, so even if I wasn't attacked by goblins," she ranted, "then I would have proof that maybe what you were saying is real. You should be happy I did instead of shouting at me."

Gripping her shoulders, I breathed in and out through my nose, swiftly losing control of my anger. "That tome isn't simply a book. It has power. It is sacred to the Historian. To you and all who came before you. If it gets damaged, it could disappear. We could lose all those years of recorded history."

"You don't have copies?"

"Copies?" I shouted, releasing her, pacing away. "No, we don't have copies. That tome will not return to the Archives until the next Historian, you —" I jabbed a finger at her. "—presents herself to the Council of Seven and accepts her destiny. You have not done that yet. And," I added, stalking toward her, "that book is a beacon for the goblins. They track its power."

"Shit," she whispered and stomped on my foot with a frustrated yell. "Why didn't you tell me that, you asshole?"

"I didn't think you were going to simply hand it over to someone."

"Well, I did. You don't have a right to be pissed since you're not the one running around with no idea what the hell is going on. That's me. Next time, maybe tell me the important shit upfront."

My brow arched at her outburst. "Are you quite finished?"

"No, not even close." Her anger slipped to worry in a split second. "Damn, they're going to be heading right for Phil."

I took hold of her hand and dragged her out the door. She would have to deal with being in blood-stained clothes for now. "Where is he?"

She directed me across campus, the rain barely a drizzle falling on our heads. We sprinted to the large stone building and through the dimly lit halls. I never let go of Nienna's hand, not about to let her out of my sight for a second. Loq and Lyz, along with their small band of warriors, weren't the only ones after Nienna. The other clans would've sent goblins to claim the new Historian. I picked up the pace, with Nienna pointing out which way to go.

We crashed through the doors and into the lab, only to be met by a horrid stench of burning flesh and death. Two bodies lay on the floor. I quickly blocked them from Nienna's sight.

"Phil," she demanded, shoving around me. "Is one of them Phil?"

"I don't know. Stay here," I ordered, but she slipped around me, rushing to the first body.

She was going to cause me headaches in the days to come, I just knew it. I rushed to join her at the first body, which was clearly not Phil. A second later, the realization of what she stared at seemed to crash into her. The blood drained from her face, and she promptly shoved me away, vomiting violently. I bent and held back her hair until she was finished. Leaving her sitting on the floor, I checked the second body, who was also not Phil, as it was a female.

"He's gone," I told her as she climbed to her feet, legs shaking.

Guilt and horror warred in her eyes, and she clung to a nearby chair. "I did this," she whispered, voice shaking. "I killed them because I brought that stupid book here. Because I'm, shit, I don't even know. Phil!" She spun wildly around, yelling his name.

There was no one else in the room, aside from the two dead bodies. Their wounds were ragged and torn—goblin blades. I scanned the room for any hint of the tome or trail of blood when I spied the dagger sticking out of the rear wall. Nienna saw it the same time I did and beat me to it.

"I can't read this," she said, shaking her head. "Alred?"

Wrenching the dagger free, I picked up the scrap of parchment, bearing a messy scribbled message. "It's in goblin language," I explained. "Says if we want the human back alive, we must deliver the Historian. Damn it. This is why you weren't supposed to let that book out of your sight."

"You didn't tell me that," she shouted right back. "You haven't told me anything except you're my Protector and I'm a Historian. I don't even know what that means. I don't know what any of this means." She sucked in a sharp breath, clutching her hand to her chest. "We have to get him back."

I nearly said Phil didn't matter, that only the tome did, but the second those words left my mouth, she'd probably do worse than stomp on my foot. "We will," I heard myself say instead. "But we have to go now."

"Go where?"

"Kenzu'grote. That's where the goblins would've taken Phil and the tome. The only way to get him back is to come with me," I said, but she was shaking her head, backing away from me. "We don't have time to argue anymore. Your path lies in my world, not this one."

"You don't understand. I'm not fit for this job or whatever. I can't, okay? I read books for a living, and I teach history. I don't fight freaking goblins. I can't be in a war," she rambled madly. "I'm not Garrick, alright? I'm nothing like him no matter what you or Mom say."

She was trying my last bit of patience. Knowing I would probably regret this later, I lunged forward and grabbed her hand. "I'm sorry," I uttered, pressing my palm to her forehead. She sighed and slumped in my arms. "Sleep, Nienna," I murmured. "Just sleep." My hand glowed softly when I pulled it away from her. A rush of exhaustion swept over me, but I pinched my arm, waking myself up. Using magic in the human realm took far more energy than it did back home.

Hoisting her into my arms, I exited the building and made my way toward the parking lot. It would take nearly a whole day to reach the doorway that would take us to Kenzu'grote. Thanks to Garrick's trips to the human world, I learned how to use a vehicle well enough to get us to where we could cross over. I came to the first decent looking truck and pressed my palm to the glass. It vanished, and I reached inside, unlocking the doors. Once Nienna was situated in the passenger seat, I hurried around and climbed in behind the wheel. After touching my hand to the dash, the truck roared to life. Thank the gods I was one of the few elves lucky enough to be born with magic.

I threw the truck in reverse, backed out of the parking spot, and drove by Nienna's apartment. I slammed on the brakes. Placing a protective enchantment on the truck, I ran back to her place, gathered fresh clothes and boots for her, and rushed back to the truck. I drove us away from campus, leaving the university and Nienna's old life far behind us.

As she slept, I fretted over everything she'd said to me, how she wasn't ready for this life. I doubted any Historian, or Protector for that matter, had been genuinely prepared when they were called. Even after carrying out his duty for so long, Garrick admitted he had days where he felt the weight of destiny pressing down on him. Days when he doubted his strength to keep going and do what was necessary to correct the balance.

Many centuries ago, the position of the Historian was less complicated. When Garrick took up the calling, he found himself amid chaos. So much needed to be righted, and it all fell to him. He spoke with me several times about how he feared he would fail. But he wasn't the one who didn't fulfill his destiny. That fault fell on me. I was told, the day I became a Protector, that the hardest part of my job would be letting the Historian go when it was his time. It wasn't in my blood to let someone die, but that was precisely what I'd done. I dreaded the moment Nienna asked about his death.

Every few seconds, I glanced at her, sleeping soundly beside me. Her face twitched, and she muttered in her sleep. I heard Phil's name and gripped the steering wheel hard. I had no right to be annoyed or jealous to hear his name on her lips. No right at all.

My only concern was getting her to safety and training her to be the new Historian.

I shifted in my seat, flipped on the radio, and focused on getting us to the doorway in one piece. The drive to what the humans called the Badlands would take us about twenty hours. The magic I used to put Nienna to sleep lasted, giving her rest she would need if she were to survive the next few days in Kenzu'grote.

In the stillness of the night with only the radio and Nienna's random murmurings, my thoughts drifted. For the last twenty-seven years, my sole purpose had been to keep Garrick alive. I had thrown myself into my calling without giving a thought to what would happen the day everything would change.

With Millie by his side, Garrick had come to me a year ago, his face drawn in confusion and anger. He said he had been shown who the next Historian would be, the first sign that his days were numbered. When he told me it was his daughter, I'd hoped he was wrong. No parent should have to condemn their child to a life filled with danger and certain death.

I hadn't wanted to accept his words. I told myself the tome would change its mind and choose someone else if only to save my friend from the heartache of knowing his only daughter would be dragged into a world at war. A world of blood and death and fighting to stay alive. Nienna was an innocent, far more than any Historian before her.

If she had Garrick's strength and Millie's bravery, they were buried deep. I worried she wouldn't find her true self at all. Long ago, I'd warned Garrick about getting involved with a human. He hadn't listened, and the moment he found out he was to be a father, I feared his actions would come back to haunt him. There would be consequences, I'd told him. That consequence now sat a foot away from me. Just as Garrick had been, she was the only person in my life that mattered. The life of a Protector was lonely, as it was meant to be. No distractions. No friends. No family. Only the oath I swore twenty-seven years ago mattered.

By the time I passed the sign for the Badlands, night had fallen, and I was anxious to get out of the confined space of the truck. I parked at the beginning of the trail and pressed my hand to Nienna's forehead to wake her. I just hoped she wasn't going to completely freak out when she realized where we were.

"We've arrived," I said as she stirred.

She yawned, stretching her arms over her head, and peered out the windshield. Her eyes narrowed then widened as she sat up in her seat. "What the hell? Where are we?"

"South Dakota."

"South Dakota?" she shouted. "Why are we in South Dakota? Did you, did you kidnap me?"

"I did what was necessary. I have fresh clothes for you if you wish to change. Then we must go." I pointed to the clothes in the backseat and climbed out of the truck.

She opened her door, slammed it shut, then she was standing in front of me, face red and hands curled at her sides.

"Do you want to stay in blood-stained clothes?"

She glanced down at herself and took a step back. "Blood. The goblins. They attacked—those bodies." She pressed a hand to her mouth but didn't vomit. "This isn't happening. It can't be happening. Shit, I'm losing it. Maybe I've already lost it. This is all a huge hallucination, and I'm in the psych ward with Mom." She let out a mad giggle and backed away.

She tripped over her feet, I caught her arm, preventing her from falling.

"You're not going crazy," I assured her. "I'm afraid this is your new reality."

"Yeah, starting to realize that. Of all creatures to exist, it had to be goblins. And elves, I guess. Elves aren't so bad, right? I mean, you seem pretty okay."

"Once upon a time, the goblins were too. Times changed." I waited and watched, wondering what was going on inside her head. She seemed to be silently arguing with herself over something.

I opened my mouth to reassure her everything was going to be okay somehow.

She covered my mouth with her hand. The action confused me, as did how warm her palm was and the weird sensation that shot through me from her touch. She glanced from me to her hand. Her brow furrowed, and she quickly lowered her hand, giving it an odd look.

"Sorry. I just uh, I need a minute. Can you give me that?"

We didn't have a minute, but I found myself nodding anyway.

She started to walk away but came back to poke me in the chest. "Still ticked at you for kidnapping me. How did you even do it?"

"Magic."

"Right, because why wouldn't magic exist since, you know, everything else apparently does." She rubbed her forehead, turning away from me. "You shouldn't have brought me here."

"You're the—"

"Yeah, so you keep saying," she cut me off, whirling around. "But I can't do anything like what Garrick did. I'm not who you think I am." She crossed her arms, plainly shutting down. "I'll go with you to get Phil back, but that's it, alright? We'll talk to this Council or whatever, and I'm sure they'll see that you and Garrick were wrong."

"We're not," I insisted.

"You don't know me," she whispered. "You don't."

She went around the truck to the passenger side and opened the back door. I watched her for a moment, debating on if I should try to convince her this was where she belonged when she yanked her shirt over her head, giving me a clear view of her in a black bra.

I forced myself to turn my back, giving her

privacy though she was too oblivious to realize what she was doing. I focused on the ground and assuring my weapons were secure in their sheaths. My neck burned, and I attempted to think of something else, anything else than the bare skin I'd just seen.

She was the Historian, and I was her Protector. No matter how attractive I found her, there could be nothing between us. There wouldn't be. Once we were back in Kenzu'grote, I'd remember that. My sole purpose was keeping her safe and upholding my promise to Garrick.

"I will keep her alive," I whispered quietly to the night, hoping Garrick could hear me.

Is that all you want? a voice whispered back to me in my mind.

I shook my head, clearing away the longings I found myself having ever since Millie had returned to Garrick. But what happened to her proved me right, sadly. Relationships in this life only led to pain and making mistakes. I would not risk the Historian's life simply because I imagined there could be more. Nienna was my charge, and she was already spoken for.

By a human, the voice reminded me. *She deserves someone better.*

"I can't," I told myself firmly. "And I won't. End of story."

I'd been alone for most of my life. Being drawn to Nienna was just my subconscious craving a connection with another being who wasn't a soldier. It wasn't the first time I felt this way, and I squashed the emotions down, hiding them away.

After a few mutterings, and a minute later, Nienna slammed the truck door shut, coming back to me. She was in denim pants that hugged her legs like a second skin. Her black boots laced up the front and went to her knees. She had on a black leather jacket, and underneath a dark green sweater with black flowers. Her hair had been pulled back into a bun. I should've paid more attention to the clothes I grabbed for her. She picked at her nails and shuffled her feet, waiting.

Her life was about to change forever, and a pang in my chest had me clearing my throat roughly, trying to make it go away. No Historian asked for their lot in life, but Nienna had grown up not knowing Kenzu'grote even existed. Once again, guilt crashed into me that I was stealing her from the human world.

"I'm ready, I guess," she said, breaking through my guilty conscience.

"Your new life will not be easy, but I'm your Protector. I will be with you every step of the way."

"I do not agree to anything, remember?"

On impulse, I took hold of her hands, stopping her from breaking any more nails. "There's more to you than you think, that I promise. Now we must go. We can discuss everything else once you're safe."

I let go of her hands reluctantly and set off into the night, weaving around dead trees and rocks. She fell in step beside me, not saying a word. I hated the fear and the doubt in her eyes, but now wasn't the time to convince her she was strong enough to pick up where Garrick left off. That would come later, if I could convince her to stay.

The hair on my neck prickled as we neared the doorway, its magic calling out to me. I paused before two tall, twisted, bent trees, jutting out from the ground at awkward angles. Their branches came together to form a woven archway. The air shimmered, the only indication there was anything there at all.

"Ready?"

Nienna swallowed hard and nodded. "Yeah, ready."

Together, we stepped to the doorway and passed

through it. A rush of cold fell over me, and she gasped beside me. Passing through the doorway always felt as if someone had dumped cold water on me. We stepped out the other side and were immediately hit but a burst of hot, dry air. This wasn't the most ideal doorway to come out at, but it had been the nearest one since Garrick forced me to the human world without a potion to get me back.

"Welcome to Kenzu'grote," I told Nienna.

"Holy shit," she whispered, eyes wide. "It's real."

I took in the burning suns overhead, raising my hand to shield my eyes from their bright rays. Several dark clouds loomed on the horizon. A storm was coming, and storms in the Plains of Frault were not easy to survive. Gusting winds blew dirt around our legs. A long time ago, these plains had been filled with grasses, a river running through them.

Then the goblins started their war, and now all that remained was dried dirt, an empty riverbed, and skeletal trees jutting out of the ground. A few structures remained of burned-out shells of timber and stone, the only indication that anyone had settled here.

"Is it all like this?" Nienna asked.

"No, but it will be soon if we can't find a way to win the war. We must keep moving."

"Where are we going?" she asked, falling in step beside me.

"To introduce you to the Council of Seven."

This was going to be a very, very long day.

Chapter 6
NIENNA

Following Alred across the wasteland, I couldn't stop trying to see everything. The direction we walked seemed random, but it was away from whatever terrible storm swiftly approached behind us. A thousand different questions were on my tongue, but I kept them to myself. Since we'd stepped through the doorway, there had been a hardness to his green eyes that hadn't been there back home. The gold flakes flared each time he glanced my way, but he never said a word.

I distracted myself from wallowing in terror from what I'd walked into by taking in my surroundings and memorizing every detail. With every step we took, I waited for panic and fear to hit me. I expected to be crippled by it all and simply fall to the ground and give up. I was in a different world. Goblins existed. Mom's rantings had all been true, and now Phil had been kidnapped. Hell, I'd been abducted, too, it seemed.

Instead of losing what little sanity I had left, the weirdest feeling that I was going home kept hitting me right in the stomach. This wasn't right; it shouldn't be. I didn't want to stay here. I wanted to go home, but the pull grew stronger with every step. I put my hand to my stomach, wondering at the pull. It felt as if someone was tugging me along.

"You're feeling the tome," Alred said, startling me. "It's calling you."

"What?"

He nodded to my stomach, where my hand was. "The tome is tied to the Historian and vice versa. Now that you're here, you can feel the pull a hundred times stronger. Magic flows far easier here than it does in the human world."

"Great, that's awesome."

He grunted, sounding aggravated. "We're nearly there."

My steps slowed. My brow wrinkled. "Wait, if I can sense where the tome is, shouldn't we just follow my gut? Then we can find it, and Phil and I get home."

"It's not that simple."

"Why not?" I closed my eyes, focusing on the tugging, and turned my feet, so I faced toward what appeared to be a grove of very tall, dead trees. They were overgrown, with twisting black vines and pointy thorns the size of my hand. I gulped and pointed. I got Phil into this mess. I was going to save his ass and get him away from those goblins. At least, I told myself that's what I was going to do, even though I wanted to run screaming in the other direction. "He's that way. Let's go."

I'd barely taken a step when a firm hand grabbed my upper arm, yanking me to a stop. "Have you lost your mind?"

"What? I need to save Phil."

"We're not going after him on our own. And that path right there? It's guarded by worse creatures than goblins."

I tore my arm free, or tried to, but Alred held on, guiding me back the direction we'd been heading. "You can let me go. I'm not a child."

"You sure about that?"

I stomped on his foot. From his lack of reaction, he hardly felt it, kept walking. "Just let me go, alright? I won't go that way."

"You're not going at all. I'm taking you to the

Council. From there, we will figure out what to do about getting the tome back."

"And Phil," I snapped.

He rolled his eyes. "And Phil." He let me go and picked up the pace. "We're close."

"Close to what?" I spread my arms wide at the vast landscape of dead trees, burned-out buildings, and nothing but gusting, hot wind hitting me in the face.

On the bright side, it was a dry heat, and I wasn't drenched in sweat beneath my leather jacket. The clouds had moved in enough to block out the two suns. Two suns, a sight I'd have never thought I'd see. As far as I could tell, we were heading toward absolutely nothing. Way, way in the distance, so far away, I believed it was a mirage, was a jagged mountain range. Between us and it, there was nothing.

"Alred, did you hear me?"

"Yes, I heard you."

"You could fill in some blanks for me, you know. I get it you're pissed I'm not going to be the Historian, but answering my questions wouldn't hurt, would it?"

"I have nothing to say to you that can't wait until we're somewhere safe."

"Right, sure, whatever."

He stopped short, and I ran right into the back of him. When he turned, he pierced me with a furious gaze that made me shut my mouth while my cheeks grew hot. "Did it even cross your mind that perhaps I'm being quiet so I can listen? There's a chance goblins will attack us out in the open. Or the dark, twisted beings that inhabit the plains will smell us and come running. As you are not a fighter with any skill to protect yourself, I have to keep us both alive. We are not in your world anymore, got it? There is an entirely different set of rules here. Rules that you will learn to follow. Am I clear?"

I planted my hands on my hips, glaring right back at him. "All this other shit might scare me, but you don't. And you don't have a right to be pissed. You weren't the one who was kidnapped."

Taking a step closer until there was hardly any space between us, his eyes darkened. He had almost a foot of height on me, and I ended up tilting my head back to hold his gaze. "I'm trying to make you see you can't pretend like this is some sort of dream. This is reality, which means you can be wounded. You can die."

"I get it."

"No, I don't think you do, not yet."

"I'm not some kid. I'm a grown woman," I ranted.

He barked a laugh.

"What? I am."

"You are a child in the eyes of elves. A sprite."

I bristled at his words and stomped on his foot again. This time, his lips thinned, but that was it. "I haven't lost it. I haven't had a breakdown. I'm here, and I'm keeping it together the best I can. All I want to do is find Phil and get home."

His eyes narrowed. "I did not bring you here to simply find Phil. You have a destiny to fulfill, whether you want to believe it or not."

I shifted on my feet, crossing my arms. "And I told you, I can't do it. Any of it."

"I didn't bring you back here so you can say no."

"Well, I am. I'm so freaking tired of everyone walking all over me and telling me what I should do or what I can do. I agreed to come with you to get Phil back, but I am not the person you're looking for." I wanted to go back home. I wanted to see Mom again and Alice. Shit, I didn't want to be hunted down by freaking goblins. Flashes of the dead bodies on campus had me swallowing back bile. My knees grew wobbly.

The hardness in Alred's eyes turned cold. He backed away. "Perhaps you're right."

The disappointment in his words stung. He agreed with me. I should've been happy, but instead, I felt empty, like someone cut open my chest and carved out a hole. I had nothing else to say and didn't try to fill the silence. Alred grunted, turned, and stormed off.

"If you don't want to get caught in that storm, I suggest you follow me."

"Then you'll help me find Phil and take us home?" I asked once I caught up to him.

"That is not my decision to make."

I fell a few steps behind him, unable to bear the blank look on his face now. I'd been content with my books and research. I loved my job at the library. Never did I think the stories Mom told me had any truth to them, or that they were about my own father. I was a half-elf coming to an entirely different world that shouldn't exist. No matter what Alred said, I belonged in the human world. Besides, I owed Garrick nothing. I owed these elves nothing.

Alred threw out his arm, and I stopped short of running into it. "We're here."

Where *here* was, I hadn't a clue. The same barren ground was beneath my boots. The air was still hot and pressing in around me. The stench that was a mix between rotting meat and eggs continued to assault my nose.

Alred scuffed his boot on the ground, revealing a set of stark white stones, three in total, each bearing a different symbol. The first stone had yellow crystals and various shaped leaves in green, red, orange. The second bore blue diamonds shaped into a wave. The third had a lance created with gold and silver gems. They formed three points of a triangle, outlined with smaller, black stones.

"What is that?"

Alred kept his mouth shut.

I crossed my arms. Great. Now he wasn't going to talk to me at all. *Way to go, Nienna.*

Alred pressed his hand to each stone in turn, and an archway appeared. It was made of stone and covered in vines bearing forest green leaves and small yellow and white flowers. Within the arch, the air shimmered, much as it had done when we passed into the Badlands.

Alred walked to it and waited.

I glanced around, but there was nowhere else I could go. I wasn't even sure how to get back home without his help. Sighing, I stepped up beside Alred. He took hold of my arm, and together, we passed through the shimmer and stepped out in a completely different place than we'd just been in.

"Wow," I whispered in awe. "It's beautiful."

"Welcome to Vel'Baram, the heart of the elven courts," Alred said. "The Council of Seven will be in the Grand Hall. They're expecting us."

I nodded absently, too busy spinning around to study the vibrant world we'd appeared in. The archway remained behind me, situated in the center of a stone courtyard.

Two elves, I assumed were guards, stood close by, pikes in their right hands, and long shields with points resting on the ground in their left. Their silver armor glinted in the pale sunlight streaming through the tree branches. Yellow and golden leaves fluttered in a breeze that soothed the heat of the plains I'd spent all day walking through with Alred.

"Nienna."

"Huh?" I whirled around to find Alred studying me with one brow arched. "What?"

He opened his mouth, but his words died on his lips when someone else yelled his name.

Another elf rushed over, dressed in white and gold robes. His long blond hair was half up, half down, and braided delicately. "My gods, you had me worried to death. I thought you weren't going to make it back. Did you find her?"

Alred nodded toward me. "Meet Nienna Havard," he said, not sounding pleased at all to be saying my name.

I wanted more than anything to disappear at that moment, wishing he never came to find me.

The elf rushed forward and took my hand.

"Oh, hi," I exclaimed and forced a smile.

He bowed over our hands. "Jurgis, at your service. I was there for Garrick, and I will be there for you, as well."

"That's—uh, that's nice," I said lamely. "Thanks, I think. Are you a Protector, too?"

"Good gracious, no," he said with a nervous laugh. "I'm a healer. Speaking of which, Alred, your shoulder. Did you let it heal before you did anything foolish to make it worse?"

His shoulder? Alred hadn't said anything about being hurt.

He grimaced.

Jurgis was suddenly at his side, poking and prodding his right shoulder.

"Leave it. I'm fine."

"From the pinched look on your face, I'd say you're not," Jurgis argued. He was as tall as Alred, but on the leaner side and had kind, gentle blue eyes that matched his soft features. "I need to look at it. I thought you were simply going to the human world."

"I was. We ran into a bit of trouble. Jurgis, enough," Alred snapped and threw up his hands, pushing Jurgis away. "You can see to it later. Nienna must be introduced to the Seven."

"I shall accompany you, then."

Alred stormed away, leaving Jurgis and me to fall in behind him. "When did he get hurt?" I asked Jurgis as we walked, keeping my voice low.

"A war band attacked our camp," he explained. "An arrow struck him in the shoulder. I'm afraid it happened right before Garrick sent him to find you." His face fell, and his hand came to rest on my shoulder. "I'm so sorry he's gone, my dear. So deeply sorry. He was a good elf."

"So I've been told. And thanks," I said, not wanting to hurt his feelings by saying I couldn't miss someone I didn't know. "Where are we, exactly?" I asked, wanting to get off the topic of Garrick.

"This is Vel'Baram. The three elven courts gather here, a neutral location, if you would. It's where our main governing body resides."

"The Seven he mentioned?"

"Precisely. Two nobles from each court reside here, the seventh member of the Council is chosen every seven years, coming from one of the three courts."

"And those are?"

"Oh, yes, of course. Goldlance. Then there is Oceanfall, the court I was born in, and lastly, Fourleaf. Your father and Alred are from that one."

Three elven courts. I vaguely remembered they were mentioned in the tome but had been too distracted by the goblins. I wasn't sure why I was bothering to learn this at all.

Jurgis kept talking, explaining how the Council ruled over the three courts and how the courts themselves worked. I half-listened, too busy admiring the unique and delicate architecture of Vel'Baram. The path we walked down was stone lined with vibrant orange and red flowers. Beyond them was a line of tall trees that stretched higher than the redwoods I used to visit with Mom. I craned my head back, straining to see the tops of them. The smooth white and ivory stone buildings were built in and around the gigantic trees. We passed through the trunk of one, and I stared up, amazed to find the entire inside was carved with a spiraling staircase and several more structures built into the heart of the tree.

"Quite a sight, is it not," Jurgis said when we came out the other side of the tree.

"Something like that."

Ahead of us was a silver gate, currently open, with two more guards posted on either side. The gate stood in the middle of a stone wall draped in more vines and flowers. Beyond it was an extensive garden overflowing with shrubs and colors I'd never have thought possible for plants. Carved statues of elven figures lined the main walkway, their delicate faces familiar and foreign at the same time. The path widened, and we came to an open area with elves milling about, talking. Most wore long, flowing dressed and robes, much like the ones Jurgis sported. I noticed only four others dressed like Alred.

"Are they Protectors?" I asked Jurgis, noting how most of the elves we passed turned to stare.

"No, they are warriors. There is only ever one Protector, just as there's only one Historian."

I took the curious looks in stride, hating how my hands became sweaty, and my nerves had started to fray. I wiped them on my jeans, concentrating on the building looming ahead of us. This one had been erected around another tree, whose shade casting a shadow over it. Leaves the size of my arm fluttered around us.

We passed through an archway. There were no doors or windows, just open spaces allowing the cooling breeze to blow freely through the corridors. Several sets of guards lined what looked like the main corridor. None of them moved an inch until we neared the only set of doors I'd seen in the whole place so far.

"State your purpose?" the guard to the right asserted loudly when we came to a stop.

"Alred Lightvale. I've brought the Historian, Nienna Havard," he announced, crossing his left arm over his chest, and bowing.

The guard lifted his spear, tapping it twice on the stone floor. "You are expected. Welcome, Historian Nienna Havard," he directed at me.

I wasn't sure if I should respond or not, but the silver and gold doors were opening, so I followed Alred and Jurgis into an open room with a raised platform at the far end. The table was curved into a crescent shape, and seven faces turned to observe at our entrance. Tapestries bearing the symbols I'd noticed on the stones earlier decorated the walls, but it wasn't this sight that set my heart to pounding.

"Nienna?" Jurgis asked. "Are you alright, my dear?"

I heard him, but my mouth wouldn't work. There, flanked by violet swaths of silk, were paintings of various elves. Their faces covered the wall. None of them smiled. I glossed over all of them except the one of the elf at the bottom. His eyes nagged at a faint memory. As did the rest of his face. His reddish-blond hair was the same shade as mine, and I knew without anyone telling me that this was Garrick. I went to the painting, delicately touching the gilded black frame. Those painted eyes held so much life and love. I backed away in a hurry and turned to find nine faces watching me closely.

Alred's brow was bunched, and he appeared torn. Whatever silent argument he was having with himself, he ended up staying where he was, arms crossed.

"Nienna Havard," one of the women at the table said. "We are pleased to see you have arrived in one piece and unharmed. I am Thalia, the seventh member of the Council."

I approached the table as she bowed in greeting.

To say she was pretty was an understatement. Her silver hair flowed over her shoulders in soft curls, complimenting the dark tone of her skin. Her silver-blue eyes shone with sympathy and something else that disappeared the longer I held her gaze. The dark violet robes she wore dragged behind her when she walked around the table and down the set of stairs, facing me.

"Nice to meet you," I said and held out my hand.

She smiled and took it. "Human and elf customs are different, but you'll adjust in time. The others of the Council also bid you welcome, but more in-depth introductions can be made later once you've settled in. I trust your journey here was uneventful?"

"Sadly, no," Alred answered for me. "We ran into goblins from the Red Wolf clan. They've been dispatched of, but we have a complication."

"And what is that?" Thalia asked.

"Aside from Alred essentially kidnapping me?" I muttered.

Thalia's brow furrowed.

Alred sighed. "It was the only way to get her here."

"I told you, I'm not this Historian, alright? Look," I said, turning back to Thalia, "my friend was taken by the goblins," I explained. "I need to get him back before they kill him."

Thalia frowned. "Why would they want your friend? He's human, yes?"

"I may have uh, left the tome with him," I replied quietly, and all seven members of the Council, along with Jurgis, gasped, as if I'd told them I smothered little kids in their sleep. "I didn't know it was wrong at the time, and I'm sorry. Can we please just do something to get him back?"

"I'm afraid it's not that simple," Thalia said, echoing Alred's earlier words. "And the tome? The goblins have it?"

"They do," Alred said. I didn't have to turn to feel his aggravated glare on me.

"That does indeed complicate matters. But for the moment, our priority is seeing you attended to. We will discuss a plan to find your friend and retrieve the tome. Until then, there is much we need to discuss, it seems. Did Alred not explain your destiny to you?"

"He did, but that doesn't change anything."

"I'm afraid it changes everything," she argued gently.

I picked at my nails until one broke, and I shoved my hands in my back pockets. "I know that

Garrick supposedly said I'm the next one, but it's not me. I might be his daughter, but I'm nothing like the elf I was told about. I have a nice, quiet, safe life back in my world, and it's where I want to stay."

Thalia blinked. "I don't understand. You were called, were you not?"

"I don't know. I mean, Alred showed up, and then there was this tome thing, and goblins tried to kill me, but I'm not sure I'm supposed to be here. I never heard a voice or felt anything change if that's what you're asking."

"Garrick saw her as the next Historian," Alred said, and I shot him a look which he returned in kind. "And the tome reacted to her touch. It has been calling to her since we arrived in Kenzu'grote."

"But I wasn't called. I'm telling you, Garrick and that damned book are wrong," I said, knowing I was grasping at straws. I frowned, remembering the dream I had and the man in that dream. No, not a man. An elf.

Thalia tilted her head, walking around me. "You just thought of something. What is it?"

"I uh, I might've had this bizarre dream the other night," I admitted. "Now that I see Garrick's face, it might've been of him. There was a fight going on of some kind, but look," I said in a rush when she nodded knowingly, "my mom told me stories about goblins all the time. I was probably just dreaming about them, right?"

Thalia studied me, coming back to stand in front. "The calling is usually a bit more forthcoming than a dream, but I believe that was the tome trying to reach you. Now that you're here where magic is stronger, the calling might yet reach you."

"Or I'm not your Historian." I pinched the bridge of my nose, telling myself not to start crying in front of a room full of strangers. "Please, I just want to get my friend back in one piece. He's in this mess because of me. Can we do that and then figure out everything else?"

Thalia turned to the six elves at the table. After a long thirty seconds of silence, they bowed, and she sighed.

"We will make finding your friend and the tome our priority," she assured me. "But while you are here, you will be treated as the next Historian. No other has come forth, and Garrick did name you his successor. I'm afraid you may be trying to run from your destiny. It's not possible."

"Can you blame me?" I muttered without thinking.

But she laughed my comment off. "No. Being the Historian is not an easy calling, but if you are anything like your father, I have faith you will succeed."

Alred shifted, seeming uncomfortable at her words. I wasn't about to point out that my own Protector thought I was nothing like dear old dad, and he was right.

Thalia clapped her hands, and the doors behind us opened.

"Now, let's put all this destiny business aside. You look as if you could use some food and good wine. I can tell you all about Kenzu'grote and Vel'Baram."

"Sounds great," I said, giving in. I was tired of arguing. And yeah, I was hungry.

As Thalia guided me to the doors, I spotted Alred standing to the side of the room, ever watchful. His eyes narrowed when he noticed I was looking his way. His shoulders tensed, and I sensed his annoyance with me. He might be my Protector, but it was damned obvious he wanted nothing to do with me.

Chapter 7
ALRED

I stood with my back to the mirror, staring at the puckered wound filled with healing salve. Jurgis had put more on it last night, and though the injury had healed, my shoulder and part of my back were stiff, making it hard to raise my arm. Gritting my teeth, I rolled my shoulder, lifted my arm as high as I could, then lowered it. After several minutes, the stiffness receded a hint.

I stalked around my chambers in the Central Tower at Vel'Baram, the place that had been my home since I was called to be Garrick's Protector. The area was open, with enough room for a sitting area in front of a stone hearth, another area with a desk and several bookcases filled with old texts, and a large bed next to a chestnut wardrobe. A small weapons rack resided on the wall beside the wardrobe. The bathroom was through a door just beyond. There were no personal touches, even after all this time. No paintings or trinkets to show who lived here, nothing aside from my muddy boots on the old red rug on the floor, and my daggers and two short swords, hanging near my bed.

"It's for the best," I reminded myself, pulling a fresh shirt from the wardrobe and gingerly slipping it over my head.

My hair was a mess. I combed my fingers through it, tugged it back into a tight plait, and grabbed my boots on my way to the door. After Thalia had taken Nienna to get settled in, I hadn't said a word to her. I'd watched over her throughout the evening and into the night, until finally, Thalia said she would let her get some rest. I'd guided Nienna to Garrick's chambers, which were now hers, and left her alone. She'd called out to me, but I kept walking.

I hadn't been in any mood to discuss her decision to not be the new Historian. I hadn't exactly expected her transition to be easy, but for her to flat-out refuse her calling? It had never been done before, and there was no hiding my disappointment that Garrick's daughter was turning out to be quite difficult. I didn't have the time or patience to deal with difficult. The dream she mentioned would've been enough to convince anyone else, but not her.

This morning, I would have to face her, but with any luck, she would be late coming down for breakfast. I had some time to figure out how to explain to her the severity of her decision. Then again, I wondered if maybe Garrick and the tome were wrong, and she wasn't the next Historian after all.

You want her to stay for more than one reason, my annoying subconscious nagged as I exited my chambers. *Admit it. There's something about her you like.*

"And plenty I don't like," I muttered.

"Alred, good morning."

I stopped and nodded to Thalia, coming down the corridor from my left. "Good morning."

"How's your shoulder healing?"

"Well, as always, when Jurgis puts his salves to it."

"Glad to hear it. And I never had a chance to say I'm sorry for your loss. Garrick's death has hit us all quite hard, but you the hardest, I'm certain of it. Soon, I hope you'll have a chance to grieve."

We walked, and I nodded solemnly, clasping my hands behind my back. "I don't think he'd want me to waste time, honestly. He'd say there was no good in it. He's dead, and it's time to move on."

"Sounds like Garrick," she commented. "I must admit, I'm a bit apprehensive about Nienna. She's not exactly who I pictured when he sent word of his daughter following in his footsteps."

"She grew up in the human world. Millie told her the truth by using fairy tales. Nienna had no reason to believe they were real until I showed up. She's coming into her destiny blind." I slowed to a stop. "Do you think there's a chance she's not who we think she is?"

Thalia studied me, resting her hand on my shoulder. "I have known you a long time, Alred, a very long time. Why do you appear so troubled?"

"She doesn't want to be here," I replied. "My worries are for the Historian, nothing more."

"Your words sound anything but sincere. There's something else, isn't there? Something about Nienna that has you on edge."

Of all the elves I'd ever met, Thalia was the best at reading people, and somedays, I hated her for it. Lying and saying I felt nothing for Nienna would be a waste of breath. Thalia would see right through my words. Nienna's constant denial infuriated me. Her lack of consideration for what Garrick died trying to accomplish aggravated me to no end. She was going to be a pain in the ass to train because of her attitude. A few times, I spotted a glimmer of the same fire that had driven Garrick, but it fizzled out quickly, overridden by her fear and uncertainty. Despite how irritated she'd made me since finding her, I sensed myself drawn to her more than as her Protector.

Roughly, I cleared my throat, going with the simplest truth I could think of. "My oath is to watch over the Historian. That is all that matters. Her lack of experience has me worried for the days ahead, if we convince her to stay."

"Hmm, partial truth," Thalia said, and I sighed. "But, your worries are understandable. I need you to speak to her today. I've told her about our world, how time passes here, the basics. But you need to explain to her how important this duty is. If she turns her back on it, she turns her back on us all. No Historian has ever refused the calling. I would hate for Garrick's daughter to be the first."

I bit back what I wanted to say, and we continued to walk toward the hall for breakfast. I sat down at one of the many long tables, nodding in greeting to the elves already gathered. Thalia joined her husband at the far end of another table. He kissed her on the cheek once she sat down, and they laughed about whatever she said.

I grunted, turning away from the scene, and poured myself a steaming cup of coffee, contemplating how I would deal with Nienna's stubbornness. I'd barely figured out what I was going to say when she appeared on the other side of the table from me, but she was not the same woman I'd walked to her chambers last night.

"Oh, good, there's coffee," she murmured, pouring herself some. "Alred? You okay?"

Over my coffee mug, I took in the changes Nienna had gone through since last night. The gold bracelet on her wrist was gone, taking the enchantment with it that hid her most prominent elf feature. Her ears.

Her pointed elf ears stuck out of the blondish red locks hanging loose around her shoulders. Those fiery green eyes of her now shone with gold flecks, shimmering in the early sunlight filling the hall. It wasn't that she hadn't been attractive before, but now my gut twisted in a way I wasn't expecting. Had to be the leather pants she was wearing, along with the black blouse and leather corset our women warriors wore. They weren't tight like the traditional human corsets but were, in truth, leather armor. Nienna went from sticking out to blending right in. She might say she didn't belong here, but her appearance and that spark in her eyes said otherwise. If she stayed in Kenzu'grote, she would thrive.

Gods, give me strength.

I was in trouble. Oath. I had to remember my oath.

"I see you're embracing your elfish side though you claim you don't wish to be here," I finally said, nodding to her ears.

She touched her pointed ear, flashing a confused grin. "Yeah. Thalia told me about the bracelet. I had no idea what those words meant."

"An enchantment to help you blend in."

"Yeah, but I figured I don't need to do that here. One of the women tried to give me a dress this morning, but I was never much for dresses. They gave me these clothes instead. Fit pretty well."

No, a dress wouldn't suit Nienna. I started to smirk, picturing her in a long flowing gown and hating it until I caught her watching me. The smirk disappeared, and I returned to my task for the day. "Once you've had breakfast, there are several items we need to discuss."

"Like getting Phil back alive?"

"We will speak with the Council again this afternoon. Hopefully, they'll have news." A heavy silence fell between us, and I struggled to find something to say that wouldn't start an argument or have her trying to stomp on my foot. Again. "Did you sleep well?"

She tucked a lock of hair behind her pointed ear, her cheeks growing red. "You could've told me those were Garrick's rooms."

"I thought I did."

"You didn't." She put her coffee down and selected a muffin from one of the platters. Instead of eating it, she picked it apart over her plate. "I found letters he wrote to Mom. Ones which, I guess, he never got to send. And I came across the ones she wrote him." The rest of the muffin crumbled onto the plate, but her eyes were focused on the table. "They spent so many years apart, and for what? So he could answer this calling? Be killed by goblins in the end?" Her voice rose, and she quickly averted her gaze when those nearby stared. Pushing her plate aside, she rested her hands on the table. Her body tensed like she was getting ready to make a run for it. After giving her head a shake, she picked up her coffee again, holding the mug so hard, her knuckles turned white.

"I think it's time you learn about your destiny."

She fumbled with her mug, nearly spilling it. Her cheeks burned brighter red. "Right. Destiny. Alred, I already told you—and them—I don't think I'm the right person for this gig."

I set my mug down harder than intended, gaining a few looks from those around us. "It's not a gig. It's a calling, a sacred duty, if you will."

"Why? You really need someone to keep track of what happens here?"

I stood abruptly. "Come along."

"I didn't finish my breakfast."

We both glanced at the destroyed muffin.

I raised my brow. "You can eat later. Right now, you need to understand what your father did and what you've been called to do."

She drained her coffee and followed me out of the hall. "I understand how important history is," she said. "It's what I went to school for. But do you really need one designated person to record it all? Why don't you have a bunch of people doing it? And why do you only have one tome or whatever at a time?"

"Centuries ago, when your world was still trying to evolve, elves and goblins had thriving civiliza-tions. We were gifted life by the old gods," I explained, winding our way down long stretches of corridors lined with paintings and tapestries. "At first, there was peace, but it didn't take long for the goblins to turn against us."

"Sounds like any other society," she commented.

"The Historian came into being," I said, ignoring her words, "to help us learn about our enemy. You see, this person doesn't simply record what has happened already. They see what will come to pass and record the events as they come."

"Wait, like a psychic?"

"Yes and no. At first, the ability allowed us to see more than mere battles. We were able to know when certain clans were on the move, or who was currently in power."

"That seems a bit unfair."

I paused, reminding myself not to lose my temper with her. She had no idea the horrors the elves had been through. "The gods had favored both races equally, but several goblin leaders took that generosity and exploited it, polluted the power they'd been granted. They manipulated the others out of greed and started a war that was never meant to happen. The elves were caught off guard and, within months, were facing defeat. The goblins were far too numerous, and the elves were constantly being pushed out of their territory. My kind was slaughtered in droves. That is why the gods granted us the Historian. To aid us without directly interfering. We could do what we pleased with the information gained from this person."

"I'm sorry," she murmured. "I didn't know it was that bad."

I nodded and set off again. She stayed by my side, and I led us to the courtyard, on through another open doorway. "The events the Historian saw happened in the near future, giving the elves time to anticipate an attack. Over the centuries, the goblins were slowly pushed back, but even still, the war takes its toll on my kin. And every major battle that takes place here affects the human world."

"What do you mean?"

"Our worlds are woven together, only separated by a fragile veil. It's why magic exists in your world but is a fragment of what it could be and is only felt by those who are sensitive to it. But natural disasters, fires, wars, all of it are influenced by dark power used by the goblins. It overflows our world and right into yours."

"Phil," she said, shaking her head, "he left me a message about the dates in the book coinciding with events back home. That's what he was talking about?"

"Yes. Smart man."

"Bad shit's going to keep happening until the war ends. Is that what you're telling me? But why were the goblins after me? If the Historian sees when they attack, there's no point unless it's just to keep the elves blind."

We came to a stop outside a set of heavy brass doors engraved with copper vines and leaves. I rested my hands on the knobs but didn't turn them. "I'm afraid it's much worse than that." The smallest part of me said to walk away and take her home now. It wasn't worth putting her through the chaos of war. She wasn't Garrick, and there was a high chance she'd break. But duty overrode everything else. I opened the doors wide and stepped aside to let Nienna enter first. "Welcome to the Archives."

Her jaw dropped as she walked into the room, her eyes flitting to the shelves lining the walls of the circular room. A spiral metal staircase followed the curvature of the wall, leading up three stories. Each shelf held tomes written by every Historian who'd ever lived. The tomes were set on small, stone pedestals, their covers facing outward with the gold lettering of the titles shimmering. Even now, the magic within them called to her, but she seemed oblivious to the tomes.

Nienna ran her fingers over the cover of the one nearest her. "Can I read them?"

"Of course. Any elf has access to the Archives, but the Historian especially so. These tomes are a part of you."

She had started to pick one up, but at my words, set it back down. She tucked her hair behind her ears, moving along the bottom shelf until she reached three empty spaces. "Where are the ones that go here?"

"The last space is for Garrick's tome. Once the new Historian has accepted the calling, his tome will be sent here, and an empty one will be given to the next writer."

"And the spaces behind it?"

I rested my shoulder against the doorframe, crossing my arms. "They were lost."

"How?"

"Ioc, leader of the Bloodied Fist clan, discovered how to manipulate the Historians."

"I don't understand. How do you manipulate a vision?"

"Historians, over time, learn to control the trances that come with the visions. They see without being fully locked in a helpless state. But Ioc kidnapped Hamon," I said, pointing to the first empty space, "and tortured him. After several months, Hamon lost the ability to control the trances. Once he was in them, Ioc whispered to him using dark magic. He interrupted the process, hijacked it, in a sense, causing the Historian to write down events and outcomes not destined to take place, changing the course of our world's history. We had no chance of winning any battle. Hamon's words sowed chaos, and Kenzu'grote was thrown out of balance."

"What happened to Hamon?" Nienna asked, resting her hand on the empty pedestal.

"He died. The next Historian was found by the goblins before my kin could get to him. They managed to save him before his end, which is how Garrick was saved from suffering the same fate." I pushed off the wall, moving to where Garrick's tome would eventually end up if we got it back. "For nearly one hundred and thirty years, your father worked to set the world right."

"Wait," Nienna said, throwing up a hand. "How many years?"

"Elves live for centuries. Some even reach a thousand. Your father was two hundred and twenty-seven when he died. Did Thalia not mention that part?"

"Nope, she left that out." Her hands went to work on her nails. "And how old are you?"

I shrugged. "One hundred and thirty-two."

"Right, of course, elves would live a really long time. It's fine, everything's fine. Sorry, go on."

She seemed anything but fine. I gave her a few more seconds to process then continued. "The balance has been slowly returning, but we're far from fixing what the goblins tainted. Your world continues to suffer for it. Until this war ends, Kenzu'grote and the human world will be at risk."

She picked at her nails again. After watching her do it last night while speaking with Thalia, and again now, I was pretty sure it was a wonder they weren't all broken already. "Can you tell me about him? Everything I know came from Mom, and she made him out to be this incredible hero. Now, I don't know what to think. Plus, those letters last night…" She trailed off, appearing as the innocent girl I'd seen that first day in Portland. "Mom told me I was like him, but I don't think I am. I want to know the truth of who he was."

I pushed off the wall, striding slowly around the room. "He was a hero, but all Historians are. He fought in many great battles, killed numerous goblins. Wielded a sword with wicked accuracy." I caught her eye and realized those weren't the parts of her father she wanted to know about. "But he was also stubborn to a fault," I told her. "And he had issues with following orders. He never wavered in the face of a fight and never turned his back on those who needed aid. He was kind to a fault, sometimes too kind. He showed mercy, where others would not. He was the bravest elf I ever met, and he was my friend." I winced at the sharp pain of loss for the elf I had yet to grieve.

"I see bits and pieces of him," she told me. "Fragments. I guess he came to visit when I was little."

I nodded. "As often as was possible and safe. But it grew too dangerous over the years, and his visits became infrequent."

"How did he meet Mom?"

"By chance. We ventured to the human world after each event, tracking what occurred there because of what was happening here. We were in Portland after a horrid storm blew in from the west, and he quite literally ran into her during a rainstorm. He told me that was the day she stole his heart, with her smile and her laugh, as they were drenched by the rain."

"You think he loved her? It sounded like it in his letters, but those were just words on paper."

I smiled softly. "He told me so enough times. It's why he continually went back to your world, and eventually, he told her the truth about everything. She took it in stride, and though I cautioned him against getting too close, he ended up binding himself to her."

"Why wouldn't you want him to be happy? He found someone to love."

My smile faltered, and my heart grew heavy. "Yes, but in another world. And she was human."

"So what? You hate humans?"

"No, but our lifespans are far longer than theirs. That alone would be enough to make any elf not choose the path your father did. But he was also the Historian. His life was filled with danger, something they both realized too late."

Nienna crossed her arms, and a flicker of that anger burning somewhere inside her appeared, the gold flecks of her eyes coming to life with it. "You didn't want them to be together."

I worked my jaw back and forth, finally

nodding. "I spent many days trying to talk Garrick out of a relationship, yes."

"Why?"

"I've told you why."

"Not really. Just because Garrick's life was dangerous doesn't mean he couldn't be happy. Besides, they made me. I wouldn't be here if he listened to you."

"You've already made it quite clear you don't want to be here anyway," I snapped.

Her arms fell, and she was back to picking at her nails. "It's a lot to deal with, alright? Give a girl a break. Not like you're making this easier for me by saying how amazing Garrick was. I can't live up to that." She glanced around at the tomes again and hung her head. "What happened to Mom when she was here?"

"What I told Garrick would happen if he brought her here to live."

"And that is what?"

I hoped to avoid this conversation, but she had the same determined look in her eyes that Garrick would get when he refused to back down. "The goblins found out who she was and raided our camp one night. They stole her away, and for several months, they held her captive. By the time we rescued her, they'd broken her mind."

"I thought you were supposed to protect her," Nienna whispered, voice shaking with anger.

"If Garrick had listened to me, she would've been safe," I argued. "Healers did their best to mend the damage, but there was too much. The safest place for her was in the human world. The Council tried to erase the memories of her time spent with the goblins, but she was too strong-willed. The memories persisted. It killed Garrick to leave her there, but he had no choice."

A range of emotions paraded across Nienna's face causing the gold flecks in her eyes to flare even brighter. She broke a nail, cursing under her breath. "You never told me."

"Told you what?"

"How Garrick died. You said he sent you through some portal or whatever to find me. How do you know he's even dead? Maybe he survived, and I could meet him. Or not meet him and let him keep doing all of this."

"He's dead."

"You keep saying that, but how do you know?"

"It's how it works. These tomes fill themselves

with pages. The day blank pages stop appearing, the Historian's time is up."

Nienna started to laugh but cut herself off quickly. "That's it? Just like that, the tome decides when they died?" She gulped, glaring at the tomes. "When I'll die?"

"That's how it's always been, yes."

"No Historian has ever died of old age?"

"Nienna," I tried, but she held up her hands, backing away from me.

"No, I can't do this. I don't want to do any this," she shouted and ran for the door. I beat her to it, and she shoved me hard, yelling for me to move. "You did this to me," she ranted when I refused to budge. "You uprooted me from my life, freaking kidnapped me, and handed me a death sentence. And you keep wondering why I don't want to accept this calling. What is wrong with you? You're not my Protector. You're a grim reaper."

"That's a bit overdramatic."

"Is it? I'm going to die whenever a book tells me I'm going to die. How is that fair? How is any of this fair?"

"It's not, and I'm sorry—"

"No, you're not," she spat. "You don't care about me. You never did. You thought you were finding Garrick's amazing, incredible daughter who'd be willing to take up the calling. Well, I'm sorry, but I'm not her. I never will be." She pushed me again, and when I refused to move, she stomped on my foot.

I grunted. She slipped past me when I shifted. She was getting better at doing that and making it hurt.

"We're not finished talking," I called after her.

She flipped me off and disappeared around the corner.

On the bright side, I found a way to draw out that fighting spirit in Nienna. On the other, I was sure I pushed her to turn down the calling for good. Thalia and the rest of the Seven weren't going to be happy with me.

Shit, I wasn't happy with me.

I gave the Archives one last glance, exited, and shut the doors behind me, the deep thudding of their closing sounded more like an omen of doom than of hope that I was doing the right thing.

———————————

Chapter 8
NIENNA

———————————

I ended up standing in a random corridor after rushing away from Alred. I meant to go back to my rooms, but I couldn't remember how to get there. I paced from one side of the hall to the other, not ready to accept the life I fell into because of Alred.

No, because of Garrick.

I yelled in frustration, wanting to go back home and pretend none of this ever happened. But people were dead, and Phil was taken by goblins. I had to get him back.

"What are you going to do?" I muttered to myself. "You can't fight. You can't do anything."

"Nienna?"

I wiped at my eyes, turning to face Jurgis. "Hey. I uh, I was just exploring."

He offered me a kind smile, squeezing my hand. "How about we take a walk? You look like you need someone to talk to."

"You're not going to tell me I'm wrong about everything?"

He chuckled, and we headed down the hall walking side by side. "Is that what Alred's been telling you? No wonder you're so upset. You know, he's a great Protector, but never was one for tact."

"You think?" I threw my hands up, cursing the elf I'd left in the Archives. "He just keeps telling me it's my calling and my duty and that I'm Garrick's daughter so that should be enough and then he drops the biggest bombshell. That freaking book is going to tell me when I die. How am I supposed to simply accept that? How?" I ranted. "I didn't grow up here. I didn't ever wonder in the back of my mind if I'd be called."

"That is true. You're taking in a lot more than any Historian before you." We left the corridor, wandered down a short set of stairs, and ended up in another garden filled with weeping willows and indigo flowers lining the stone path. "But his sole purpose for the last twenty-seven years has been to follow his own calling, which means protecting his charge."

"Didn't he have a life before, though?"

Jurgis held his arm out, letting the branches glide over his skin. "Alred comes from a long line of warriors. Since he was old enough to hold a sword, that's all he's trained for. He fought alongside the knights in numerous battles before he was called to be the Protector."

"So, no, he had no life. That's awesome."

Jurgis laughed. "If that's how you want to see it, then I guess no, he hasn't. His parents have both passed, and he had no siblings."

"What about friends or I don't know, a girlfriend?"

When Jurgis' eyes darkened a hint, I worried I was asking too many questions. "Aside from Garrick, I'm one of the few friends he's had, and even that's a stretch. And as far as I know, he's never had a woman in his life."

"Why the hell not? Might help him ease up a bit." I ran my fingers over the silky petals of a nearby flower. "He didn't want Garrick and my mother to be together."

"Did he tell you why?"

"Yeah, danger and all that lovely life and death crap."

"Did he also tell you he was jealous of them?"

I paused, letting Jurgis get a few steps ahead of me. "You're serious? Why?"

"He never told me, but I think Alred's been lonely for many decades. He took an oath to carry out his duty, no matter what the cost." Jurgis sighed, sitting on a stone bench beneath one of the willows. He leaned back, staring into its swaying branches. "That cost is his happiness and a chance to have what Garrick was lucky enough to find."

"Love? Is there some rule that he can't have a relationship?"

"It's his rule, has been for as long as I've known him."

The realization that Alred had been alone without someone to love hit me harder than I thought it would. I had Mom, Alice, and Phil. Granted, I just broke up with Phil, but we had shared something special for a while. Alred though, he had no one. I shook my head and sank onto the bench beside Jurgis.

"Just because he's choosing to be unhappy doesn't give him the right to mess up my life."

"You truly think he doesn't care?"

"He knocked me out, Jurgis. He put me to sleep and dragged me here. No, I don't think he cares," I muttered, picking a leaf off the arm of the bench, slowly tearing it to pieces. "He made it quite clear how disappointed he is that I'm not more like Garrick. He can say it's my calling and destiny all he wants, but that won't change who I am."

"Tell me," he said, shifting so he could look at me, "who are you, Nienna Havard?"

I paused in destroying the leaf. "I'm a grad student studying history," I replied. "And a TA and a librarian. That's who I am."

"No, those are your jobs. Who are you?"

I wasn't sure what he expected me to say. "I'm not going to admit I'm the Historian."

"Also, not what I'm asking."

"Then what do you want me to say?"

"I want you to look deep, deeper than you ever have before, and tell me who you are."

I started to answer, but stopped, not even sure what to say. Until a few days ago, I knew what I wanted to do with my life. I had goals. Now everything had changed. I was part elf, and my dad was this great hero. Everyone kept telling me I had some grand destiny, but all I felt was fear. Once again, I was being pushed into doing something without having a chance to figure out if it was what I wanted.

"I'm scared," I confessed. "I'm terrified, actually."

"What else?"

I resumed shredding the leaf, unsure what I was supposed to say. "I thought I was strong, but I think after Mom left, something inside me was too busy worrying about her to stay that way. I stopped paying attention to my own life. I sort of let everyone else guide me, and I just let it happen." I threw the bits of the leaf off my lap one by one, watching them flutter to the ground. "I've been told I help everyone else too much instead of taking care of myself." That was something Mom always warned me about when I was growing up. Too bad, I didn't listen. It was probably why I hadn't broken up with Phil sooner. I spent so much energy on watching out for Alice and ensuring Phil was happy, I never stopped to focus on myself.

"Sounds like you share some traits with Garrick after all." Jurgis patted my hand. "He too cared for others so much it drove Alred mad. If there was a battle, he saw everyone else's wounds tended to before his own. He went out of his way to help those afflicted by the war, even if it meant going without food or sleep. He was a warrior, yes, but he had heart." He smiled softly. "He saved my life once, risked himself to save me, a stranger at the time."

"He did?"

"Yes, just as he did for so many others."

I slumped on the bench. "But that's just it. I don't think I can save anyone. I doubt Garrick ever let his fear get the better of him."

"Every person feels fear in the face of danger. Every person, including Alred and Garrick. They learned how to handle it. One day, you will too."

I stood, moving toward the base of the tree and rested my shoulder against the bark. "What if I don't? What if I fail? I don't feel like I'm destined for anything."

"Have you ever taken the time to listen?"

"Listen to what?"

"Destiny." He joined me near the tree. "I want you to close your eyes." I scowled, but he merely smiled. "Close your eyes. Trust me."

I did as he asked and waited. "Now what?"

"I want you to focus on your breathing and on the beating of your heart. Can you do that?"

I breathed in deep, held it, and let it out. "Easy enough."

"Shift your focus slightly. Feel the breeze on

your cheeks, hear the leaves rustling in the trees, sense the presence of the tree."

"Really?"

"Every living thing has a presence, a pulse," he explained. "It's through those connections destiny calls to us. Listen, Nienna, just listen."

Part of me thought he was full of it, but I did what he said and focused on the tree. After a minute, the strangest sensation that the tree breathed with me had my eyes flying open.

Jurgis was close by, giving me a knowing smile.

I shut my eyes again and waited to feel the pulse again. When it came, I focused on it. My heart beat in time with the pulse I realized had to be coming from the tree. A subtle vibration beneath my feet caught me off guard, but my eyes stayed closed. The breeze blew my hair, making it tickle my cheeks. Bit by bit, my fear slipped out of reach, and a calmness fell over me instead. Within it was the same feeling I'd had of coming home when Alred first led me through the doorway. Warmth flowed over me, and the quietest of whispers brushed against my ear.

The words were foreign to me, but somehow, I knew they were elvish. The voice grew louder, and it was like someone lit a fire inside me. A flood of images flashed through my mind, too fast for me to focus on any single one. The voice shifted and changed, sounding male.

Nienna.

I gasped, hearing my name, and grabbed hold of the tree with my right hand. *Garrick?*

Nienna, this is your time, my daughter. Trust yourself. Trust who you are.

I don't know who I am.

You will learn.

For just a second, a warm hand cupped my cheek. It faded in the span of a heartbeat, and I let out a breath, opening my eyes. My cheeks were wet. For a split second, I caught sight of Jurgis, then a sharp pain shot across my forehead. I crashed to the grass on my knees, gasping for air.

An explosion of scenes played out in my mind. Elves and goblins were locked in a fierce battle. Shouts and yells of the dying assaulted my ears. A firm hand grabbed hold of mine. An arm closed around my shoulders. I sank into that warmth, waiting for the agony to end. Faces went in and out of focus until a familiar voice shouted above all the others. Flames spread around him, but he fought on, yelling for someone.

Yelling for me.

"Alred?"

My lips moved, but I had no idea if any sound came out. I strained to keep him in focus, watching as he killed goblins in a continual charge for him. My gaze shifted, and there amid the chaos was me; only it wasn't me. The elf thrusting her sword into the air letting loose a battle cry couldn't be me, could it? Alred reached her, and they fought back to back, the world burning and the goblins swarming, blocking them from view.

The vision faded, and I slumped into something solid. Two voices pierced my ears, and I cringed, trying to turn away from them.

"Alred?" I blinked against the bright sunlight to find him looking down at me, his brow creased with worry, the gold shimmering wildly in his eyes. My cheek rested against his chest, and it was his arms around me as we sat on the ground. Or rather, he was on the ground, and I was quite firmly planted in his lap.

He smoothed my hair from my face, letting out a heavy sigh. "Gods, are you alright?"

"I think so. What the hell was that? Why are you even out here?" I tried to get out of his hold, but my legs shook, and my body refused to cooperate.

"Just sit for a minute, catch your breath."

I pressed my hand to my forehead, wincing at the lingering pain. "Shit, that hurts."

"I'll get you something for the pain once you're inside," Jurgis said, crouching in front of us.

I was still trying to understand what just happened. I was doing what Jurgis said then that voice. "Garrick," I whispered, sitting upright so fast I smacked Alred in the chin with my head. "Damn it, sorry."

"It's fine," he muttered. "What about Garrick?"

"He spoke to me. Then I saw everything." There was no other way to describe it. I glanced from Alred to Jurgis, waiting for one of them to say something. Alred's face went utterly blank, but Jurgis grinned. "What?"

"The calling," Jurgis told me excitedly. "You had it."

I slumped in Alred's arms. "You're sure?"

"Yes," Alred replied this time, his tone failing to mask a hint of disappointment. Guess I wasn't the only one secretly wishing I wasn't the Historian. "I'm afraid no matter what you feel, you are where you're supposed to be. There's no more denying it."

"The hell there isn't." I pushed against his arms and chest, eventually making it to my feet.

"Nienna," Alred said, but I pressed my hand to his mouth. His careful blank expression turned to a worried frown. Jurgis' question came back to me as to whether I honestly believed Alred didn't care for me. I'd been in pain, and he was suddenly at my side. I guess he could've simply been coming to find me, but the brightness of those gold flecks told me he had sensed the agony I'd been in.

"Just because I saw something doesn't prove anything." I dropped my hand and backed away. "It can't."

"Garrick and the tome have spoken. This is your path now, but you're not alone," Alred assured me. "You will never be alone."

"Too bad you can't save me in the end, right?" I snapped furiously.

He reached for me, but his hand fell. "That day is many years off. I'm certain of it."

"That's all you're going to say?"

"There's nothing else to say," he murmured, and the little bit of hope I held onto that, somehow, I'd convince Alred I wasn't the Historian slipped out of reach. "The sooner you accept your destiny and stop doubting yourself, the sooner you can become who you're meant to be."

"You don't have a certain death hanging over

your head." I stormed past him, shoving into his shoulder on the way.

"Nienna."

"What?" I yelled. "Just leave me alone."

"The Seven are summoning us."

I whirled around, ready to tell him exactly what I thought of the Seven right then, only to find Thalia headed our way. I bit back the words I'd probably regret since these were the same people who were going to help me get Phil back. The second we told them about my finally getting the calling, I was done for. Jurgis was speaking with Thalia after I made my way back to Alred's side. We followed the two elves through the garden.

"How did you know?"

Alred's gaze slid to me. "Know what?"

"That I was having a vision like that. That I was in pain."

"It's part of being a Protector. I sense when you are in pain or in danger."

"Oh, guess that makes sense." Why did I sound so disappointed? Did I really want it to be because he felt something for me? I shook my head and figured his being able to know when I was in trouble was a good thing since it looked like I was going to be stuck here.

"Nienna? What did you see?"

I thought of the vivid vision I saw last, the one of the two of us fighting together. The woman in those images frightened me, seeing what I could turn into or would. "Just lots of fighting," I lied. "Nothing specific. Is that what happens during the calling?"

"Garrick mentioned something similar happening to him." His eyes narrowing, he added, "I thought you said my name, while you saw these images."

I forced my hands to stay at my sides so I wouldn't pick at my nails. "Weird. I didn't see you at all."

His grunt said he didn't believe me, but he left it alone.

We were led, not to the Grand Hall, where we met the Seven before, but a smaller room with a large table in the center. The rest of the Council, along with elves dressed in silver armor and emblems on their chests, stood around it. A map was laid atop the table with several small figurines in various places. Absently, I realized this must be the war room, and another piece of my old, quiet life of living in the library shattered. War. They were in the middle of a war.

No, not they. We.

"We've tracked the goblins who took your friend," Thalia told me, motioning me toward the table Alred was already standing at. I was a bit slower to approach but finally did. "They've gone through the Hollow, taking the western route toward the Red Wolf territory."

"The Hollow," Alred spat. "Of course, they did."

"Is that bad?" I asked.

"Yes," Alred replied, glaring at the map. "Taking that route, reaching Red Wolf territory will take a week, perhaps longer. We might be able to catch up to them if we cut through the marshes. Not the most pleasant path to take, but it might be our only chance. If they get much further, they'll be too close to the main Red Wolf encampment to attack."

"Agreed," another elf said. She held a helm under her right arm, using her left hand to point out the passage we would take. "My scouts have already set out to ensure the route is clear of any major threats. I'm giving you command of twenty soldiers. It's all I can spare."

"Thank you, Commander. It'll be enough, and hopefully, I'll bring them all back alive."

"You'll leave within the hour." The Commander bowed and exited the room with four elves in matching armor following close behind.

"You'll get your friend back," Thalia assured me. "And the tome."

Alred said he was going to prepare for our trip and left with Jurgis. I stayed with Thalia and the Council. The vision I had of Alred and me tugged at my mind until I thought I was going to burst.

"Can I talk to you alone for a minute?" I asked Thalia.

She waved for me to follow her to the far corner of the room. "Is this about what happened out in the garden?"

"Pretty much." I scratched at my head, mumbling, "I finally had my calling."

"That is wonderful news," she exclaimed, but when I kept frowning, she sighed. "I understand the weight this must place on your shoulders, but nothing is holding you back now. You are the next Historian, and I have faith you will finish what Garrick started."

"That's just it. I saw a lot of shit when it happened. Fighting and goblins and elves. Alred said, that's normal."

"It's the past Historians speaking to you the best they can. Did you hear Garrick?"

"I did, but it wasn't for very long."

"The missing tome could be why. Garrick said the same thing happened to him when he became Historian."

I fiddled with my blouse sleeves. "Did he also see some crazy vision of the future?"

"Nienna, what's troubling you?"

"The vision I had at the end wasn't something that was going to happen soon. It's just not possible, and what I saw," I paused, shaking my head, recalling the way I'd looked as I killed goblins mercilessly, "it was Alred and me fighting."

Thalia's gaze turned thoughtful. "Tell me everything you remember."

I started with what Jurgis was trying to show me, not sure what exactly Thalia needed to hear. I rambled about feeling the pulse within the tree, the sharp pain in my head, the images flying by. I told her what little Garrick said to me, and when I came to the vision, I lowered my voice, and my hands shook until I crossed my arms. When I finished, ending with the fire spreading, and Alred and I surrounded with no apparent way out, Thalia's face was set with confusion that quickly gave way to concern.

"Thalia?"

"I wish I could tell you what you went through was normal, but that final vision, that is not something you should have seen, not this early."

"Great. Barely the Historian for thirty minutes, and I'm already messing up."

"No," she insisted. "This power to see comes from our gods. They may be showing you this vision for a reason, but what that is, I'm not certain."

"I am. Telling me that no matter what I do, I'm going to fail, right? I'm going to die and take Alred right down with me." Dead. I was going to be dead in what, months? Maybe a couple of years? I clenched my jaw to stop myself from losing it in front of Thalia.

"They could also be showing you this, so you understand what's at stake. I don't feel this vision will come to pass. No future is set in stone."

"But the tome—"

"Never shows outcomes," she reminded me. "And though it's rare, there have been times when the Historian saw something that did not happen. The subtlest of changes, one person making one different choice, these can shift the course of the future." She rested her hands on my shoulders and smiled. "There is no reason to despair."

"Not what your eyes say."

Thalia's smile fell, and the encroaching fear in those silver-blue eyes grew. "Your father was good at that, too, seeing the truth. Now, you must make ready to leave."

"Should I tell Alred what I saw?"

"That is a decision you must make as the Historian." She placed her hand atop my head and closed her eyes. "May the gods guide you, Nienna Havard, and bring you back to us." Her hand warmed, and it was like Mom stood there beside me, wrapping me up in her favorite warm, plaid blanket. I closed my eyes at the sensation of home, and a tear slipped from my eye. Thalia removed her hand, but the feeling lingered.

"What was that?"

"Blessings. The gods believe in you."

"Too bad, I don't," I confessed. "And neither does Alred."

"I don't believe that to be true."

"Really? Tell that to the disappointed looks he's been giving me since he met me." I wanted the sensation of being home to come back, but a cold sank into my body instead.

"You both have been through much these last few days. He must adapt to his new charge, and you have to learn what it means to be in our world." She clasped her hands in front of her, but there was no smile on her face now. "You two will make this work. You just have to give each other a chance."

"And if we can't?"

"Then you both will suffer for it. You two share a bond now. Fighting it will only weaken it, and if it's weak, your life will be in even more danger." Her gaze flicked behind me, and she nodded at whoever was there. "Time to go. We can speak more when you return."

I took the dismissal, not happy about what she'd said, and turned to find Alred waiting for me in the doorway. He held a black leather overcoat in his hands and nodded at me when I approached. He offered me the coat and, without another word, headed down the corridor.

I slipped on the coat and followed, dreading how the next few days were going to play out.

That damned vision of the two of us fighting a horde of goblins haunted me every step of the way.

Chapter 9

ALRED

I grunted, swatting at another mosquito on my hand. We'd been traveling for two days through the marshes, eaten alive by mosquitos, and up to our knees in stinking muck and grime. Despite the difficult terrain and the lack of sleep since there was nowhere to make camp here, Nienna remained silent. Aside from a few uttered curses, she kept her complaints to herself and anything else that was on her mind.

On our first day, I'd asked her what she and Thalia spoke about. She'd averted her gaze and told me it wasn't anything important. She was lying. Secrets between a Protector and Historian were never a good thing. They weakened the bond. Once we made camp, I planned on asking her again, and hopefully, take care of a few other issues that needed to be addressed.

"Is that it?" Nienna asked several hours before dusk when we reached the edge of the marshes.

"Yes. Solid ground from here on out." I pointed northeast where shadows loomed within the darkness of the Hollow. "We'll follow this trail for another two days. It'll lead us to the northern edge of the wood."

"Why didn't we just go through the Hollow?"

"That wood is sick, poisoned," I explained. "The creatures within it have mutated. Nothing but insects and snakes reside in the marshes, but as for the Hollow, very few who venture in ever make it out alive."

"Then why would the goblins take that path?"

"They're the ones who poisoned the wood." I spat on the ground, cursing their clans. "The creatures leave them alone. Come, we need to make it a bit further, then we can make camp."

She nodded, shoving loose strands hair from her face. There were bags under her eyes, and she moved a bit slower, but otherwise, the lack of sleep appeared not to bother her. The twenty warriors, led by Captain Trolian, spread out in a long line, guarding our backs and flanks as we neared several jagged, rocky hills.

Between the marshes and the Hollow were more barren wastelands. There was no storm on the horizon tonight, so camping there would be safe enough. The hills would give us shelter from the wind, and the top of the hills gave us a full three-sixty view of the surrounding area. If an attack happened, we'd see it coming.

Once I called a halt, the warriors split into two groups. One set up a perimeter while the other helped make camp. Nienna offered her assistance. Though she had to be instructed, she was able to build a fire, assist in setting up the few tents we'd brought, and she helped pass out water and food before she had any herself.

"You need to eat, too," I instructed, sitting her down by the fire. "Here."

She stared at the hunk of bread and cheese. "I'm not hungry."

"You are, you just don't realize it. Eat."

"Aren't you going to have any?"

"My duty is to take care of you, since clearly, you'd rather ignore your own needs," I muttered. "Something else you have in common with Garrick."

She glowered at me and set the food aside. "Don't do that."

"Do what?"

"Keep acting like you know who I am because of Garrick. And why can't I help set up camp? Make sure everyone else is taken care of, too?"

"You can, but your life is more important. These warriors understand that."

She mocked me, parroting my words, and two elves nearby stifled their laughter.

"I might be the Historian, and I know there's shit I have to learn, but you can't change who I am. I know I'm not a great warrior like Garrick, but just, never mind."

"What?" I pushed, watching her pick at the bread, still not eating.

"What if I disappear?"

I frowned, but the fear in her words made me sit down on the hard ground beside her. "The goblins will not steal you away."

"No, I mean, what if who I am just poofs! Goes away like it never existed?"

"All people have to adjust when they become the Historian," I said slowly, not sure I understood where this concern was coming from. "Is this about you not thinking you can be a warrior?"

"No." She finally ate a bit of the bread she'd torn off, staring into the fire. The flames flickered in her eyes, and she ate a few more bites before setting it aside. I grunted, and she slid me a sideways glance. "What? I ate."

"Barely."

"I don't see you eating."

"I will once I know you're taken care of."

She rolled her eyes. "This is going to be a thing, isn't it? You, driving me crazy."

"If you would listen, I wouldn't drive you crazy." I picked up the food she hadn't eaten and placed it back in her lap. "Finish that. I'll be back after I check in with the watch." I started to walk away

Turmoil wracked her face. Her lip twitched, and she sighed heavily, like she was closing in on herself. I was about to say her name but thought better of it and kept moving.

Whatever she had seen back in Vel'Baram had stirred up a whirlwind of worry. I saw it every time she looked at me or stared off into the distance like she was contemplating how she'd ended up in this mess. Her anger toward me had faded, but I hoped to pull on that very anger. She'd need it to find that inner fire, and without her anger to bring it to life, I wasn't sure what else Nienna had. These fears and doubts would drag her down and make her weak.

I spoke with the warriors at the perimeter, hoping all was quiet.

Distant howls echoed across the wasteland. The wolves were on the hunt tonight; they'd steer clear of the fire, though. I returned to the center of camp to find the warriors regaling Nienna with stories of past battles. She leaned forward while she listened, eyes wide. The firelight brought out the various shades of reds in her hair, highlighting the soft curve of her cheek. She'd removed her overcoat and the leather corset to get comfortable. A subtle breeze lazily blew through camp, pushing the delicate fabric against her body. My neck grew hot, and I cleared my throat loudly, putting an end to the stories.

"Enough of that," I said and held out my hand for Nienna's. "We're in the wilds now. Time to start your training."

"Training?" She put her hand in mine, and I hauled her to her feet. "I don't have the tome."

"This isn't about being a Historian. This is about you learning to defend yourself."

"With a sword?" she exclaimed, watching me borrow one from a warrior nearby. "Alred, seriously, the only knife I've used in my life is a kitchen knife. And a box knife, I guess, but not a sword. I can't."

"You can, and you will."

"I thought that's why you're here."

I held out the short sword to her, hilt first, and waited. "There's always a chance I won't be."

At my words, she gulped, and her gaze took on a faraway look for a split second. She bit her lip and stepped back. "I don't want to."

"You don't have a choice. Any of these elves will tell you using a sword is what it takes to survive in our world. I'm not saying you're going to be thrust into battle, but I will not have you be completely defenseless. Every Historian before you could handle a blade."

"I'm not them," she whispered. "Alred, please."

"Take the sword, Nienna."

She gave me one last pleading look. When I continued to hold the sword out, she finally grasped it in her palm, holding it like it were about to bite her. I drew my sword from its sheath and stood at the ready; only she remained perfectly still. Sighing and reminding myself to be patient, I adjusted her hand on the hilt. I stood behind her, using my foot to move hers to the right positioning.

The calming scent of honeysuckle teased my

nose. Having her this close to me had my heart pounding, and I promptly moved away, walking around to face her.

"Your sword needs to become an extension of your arm," I instructed. "It's a part of you. When you defend or attack, you use your whole body."

"Uh-huh," she replied.

I decided a trial by fire might be the best way to teach her. If nothing else, it would shake her out of overthinking what she was doing. I swung my short sword loosely in my hand and lunged forward. She yelped and raised her sword to block me. Our swords clanged together, but she hardly put up a fight. She backed away, lowering her blade.

"You have to keep up your guard," I said and went after her again.

She glared at me but managed to block my second and third attacks. "This isn't teaching me anything," she snapped.

"It's teaching you far more than you realize." I swung wide, and she scrambled away instead of blocking. "Listen to your instincts. Fight back. The goblins aren't going to show you any mercy. If they have the chance, they will attack you, and they will kill you." I stalked toward her, swinging my sword again. She brought up her blade but continued to back up. "Fight back, Nienna."

In two quick moves, I had her disarmed and my sword at her throat, my other arm wrapped around her waist, holding her close.

She froze, but alongside the fear and aggravation on her face was the slightest bit of anger.

"Asshole," she spat.

I pushed her back. "Pick up your sword."

She crossed her arms and opened her mouth, probably to yell at me, but I charged forward. She cursed, hit the ground, picked up her sword, and managed to hold onto it longer this round.

Every time I knocked it from her hands, I ordered her to pick it up and start again. And each time, a bit more of that inner fire shown through. The gold flecks in her eyes came to life, and she yelled when she attacked me, instead of merely defending. She was a long way from being able to fight, but now I was sure she could hold her own for a few minutes.

I kicked out her feet, and she hit the ground with a grunt, breathing hard. "You did well," I said and held out my hand. "We'll pick this up again tomorrow."

She swatted my hand aside. "What's the point?"

"The point is with practice, you'll get better."

"And if I don't want to get better?"

"I'm afraid you don't have a choice."

She brushed the dirt from her pants once she was on her feet. "Just like I haven't had a choice about anything else."

"If you would trust yourself, stop doubting your abilities—"

"Then what? I can finally not be a disappointment? I can be just like Garrick?" The anger I'd stirred inside her dimmed. The same expression she had on her face when I asked about her vision returned, and she frantically picked at her nails. "We should both just get used to not getting what we want," she murmured and marched to her tent.

I stayed right where I was, debating trying to talk to her more when steps sounded behind me.

"You're hard on her," Trolian stated. His face was hard, and his blue eyes cold from decades at war. His black hair was braided close to his head and trailed down his back. Two tattoos marked his right cheek, symbols of bravery and heart.

"Not hard enough."

"She needs time. She wasn't raised as we were."

I sheathed my sword and handed the other back to its rightful owner. "I don't think we have time."

"What do you mean?"

"Don't you feel it?" I asked, taking a spot by the fire. "The air's changing. The whole world seems off as if it's holding its breath, waiting for the storm to hit."

"Every new Historian brings a change."

"Not like this. The moment I brought Nienna here, it's like I'm standing on the edge of a cliff, waiting to be pushed over. The war, the goblins, us, everything is being thrown out of balance even more than before. I fear Garrick's work is being undone."

He clapped me on the back. "Or you're simply paranoid. You lost the one you were charged with safeguarding. It's enough to mess up any Protector."

I gritted my teeth, tossing small pebbles into the fire. "I swore to Garrick I'd keep his daughter safe. How am I supposed to do that if she refuses to fight for herself? Refuses to fully give in to the calling?"

"Talking to her might be better than charging her down with a blade," he suggested. "Get some sleep. We'll leave before dawn."

I laid down by the fire, using my arms as a pillow, and stared up at the night sky, void of starlight. Since these lands had fallen to the goblins, the stars had refused to shine here. I shut my eyes, listening to the far-off howling of the wolves, and planned on how to make Nienna see her true potential before it was too late.

***

Nienna pushed off the ground and came at me, her sword swinging. We'd been going at it for a couple of hours since making camp. She was getting better by the day. By tomorrow, we should be caught up to the goblins exiting the Hollow.

"That's it?" I yelled, grabbing Nienna's wrist and easily shoving her away from me.

"I hate you," she muttered and came at me with a wild attack.

I knocked her blade aside and tripped her, sending her sprawling to the dirt. She shouted, clawing her way to her feet. "If you hate me, then use it," I ordered. "Dig deep, deeper than you have before. Let your instincts take over. Stop doubting yourself."

"If you tell me to stop doubting myself one more time, I'm going to strangle you."

"Prove it." We circled, the warriors watching from nearby. Trolian shook his head, but I ignored him. He could give me suggestions when he was the one dealing with a difficult Historian. "Right now, you can't even throw me off balance."

A flicker of anger came to life in Nienna's eyes, but she didn't attack.

"Maybe you're right. The tome shouldn't have chosen you. You're not strong enough to handle the calling," I went on. Nienna's lip twitched, and she shifted her hands on the hilt of her blade.

"It's not going to work."

I stilled at her words. "What's not?"

"You trying to piss me off. To make me angry in hopes it's going to stir up something great inside me, turn me into someone who wants to fight. You can insult me all you want, but I'm not an idiot." She lowered her sword, turning her back on me.

"No, but you are a disappointment," I called, knowing full well it was a low blow.

Nienna stopped mid-step, her shoulders tensing.

"That's what you think everyone sees," I accused.

"I don't think it, I know." She glared at me over her shoulder. "You went to the human world to find some great hero, and instead, you got me. Someone who's never had a chance to figure out who she is before she was stolen from her life. You haven't been able to hide your disappointment since the moment you told me the truth."

I clenched my jaw, and she gave a bitter laugh.

"You can't even deny it."

"You want me to admit I was aggravated to find you instead of the person I made you out to be? Fine, I admit it."

She shrugged. "And there it is, everyone. My own Protector, who dragged my ass here in the first place, doesn't even think I'm cut out for this life. And you're supposed to be my what? Mentor? Teacher? My freaking guide? Great job, really, you're doing awesome."

"I was wrong," I said, slowly walking to her. "And so are you."

"You don't have to lie."

"I'm not lying. You think you're weak, and yes, I did too, but there's something inside you, and it wants to get out. A fire, a passion to fight. To live. Maybe anger isn't what drives you, but something sparks that light in your eyes. All you have to do is see that for yourself. If you want to figure out who you are, then do it."

"How am I supposed to do that when everyone keeps deciding for me," she yelled. "You all thrust that damned title on me, and now it's who I am."

She held her blade in front of her face. "I'm so confused and overwhelmed, but I don't get time to figure all this out. I'm just tossed into the deep end while everyone tells me to be this new person without explaining how."

I was at a loss for what to say. She was right, and I hated myself all over again for bringing her here. I condemned her to this life. If I'd never found her, we would be without a Historian, but Nienna would still be living her quiet, simple, safe life.

"You might not be able to run from your destiny," I finally said, "but you are still in control of who you are. Yes, you must adapt and grow, but no one wants you to lose yourself."

"You want me to fight. To kill goblins."

"Sadly, it's a part of life here. Being the Historian means being a soldier in this war."

"Why? So I can turn into some coldhearted killer?" she shouted. "A ruthless killer with cold eyes? Is that what you want me to be?"

I frowned. "What are you talking about?"

The sword shook in her trembling hand. "This is the first step down that road, and I won't do it." She stormed away from camp and into a copse of dead trees nearby.

I cursed and went after her, not about to let her wander. "Nienna."

"Leave me alone," she threw over her shoulder, swatting at shrubs and low hanging branches with her sword. "Just go away."

I kept her in sight, hustling to keep up with her as she moved further away from the torchlight of our camp. She cursed and muttered about messing everything up. I caught up with her as she started hacking away at a wall of hanging gnarled vines blocking her path. Her mutterings turned into a furious shout, her anger and fears finally getting the better of her. For the last few days, I waited for her to have that mental breakdown. Her arms went limp, and the sword fell to the ground at her feet.

"Why did it have to be me?" she whispered. "Why?"

"No one knows why they're called. But we are, and all we can do is try to fulfill our destiny the best we can."

"Says the elf who's a badass with a sword."

Scowling, I went to her, picked up the sword, and offered it to her. When she refused to take it, I took her hand and placed it around the hilt. "It has taken me over a hundred years to become what I am, and I'm far from perfect." My hand remained around hers, enjoying the feel of her skin against mine. I told myself it was the bond we had as Historian and Protector, but the ache in my chest said it was more. "I know I'm pushing you, and it's not fair. None of this is, but if you don't find a way to make this work, the balance will never be righted, and the war will continue to get worse. You will find your strength, I promise you. You won't be a pushover then."

"You know as far as pep talks go, yours suck." She softened her words with a smile.

I squeezed her hand. "I'll try to work on that. Garrick was never a fan of them either."

"Gee, I wonder why. The whole doom and gloom shit kind of gets old."

"I never was one for sugarcoating the truth."

"I guess that's a good thing." She shifted on her feet when I removed a few leaves from her hair. She closed the distance between us, her brow furrowing. "Alred—"

A stick cracked behind her.

I stilled.

Her eyes widened. Squinting into the shadows of the trees, I searched for what had caused the noise, praying it was an animal. When a second crack sounded from too damned close, I grabbed

Nienna and tugged her down, shielding her with my body.

An arrow thudded into the trunk of a tree nearby.

"Run!" I pushed her ahead of me and took off after her.

A goblin's furious yell burst through the trees. The call was echoed by three more, and arrows struck the trees and ground, nearly hitting us while we ran. The second we reached camp, the warriors closed ranks behind us.

I pushed Nienna toward her tent. "Stay behind me, understand? And stay low."

She nodded, holding her sword, taking up the defensive stance just as I taught her.

I drew my dagger and waited, the goblins' howls closer and closer. Arrows hit the dirt, missing their targets. The warriors closed in even tighter, following Trolian's lead, readying their swords and shields, waiting.

But as quickly as the goblins' calls came, they stopped, and dead silence fell in their wake.

"Alred?" Nienna whispered from behind me, voice shaking.

"Don't move." I took a step forward, then

another, searching the darkness surrounding us for any sign of shifting shadows.

An elf let out a surprised shout as he was thrown to the ground and dragged off into the darkness.

Chains rattled.

A second elf was dragged off.

A third.

The rest of the elves closed ranks.

I moved until I stood right beside the fire.

Trolian caught my eye and nodded. He crouched, and the rest of the elves followed suit. I held out my hand with the dagger over the flames, seeking out the pulse of crackling embers. The flames grew, stretching around the blade. The heat pressed against my hand, and I bit my lip against the pain.

The fire grew wilder, eager to be unleashed. The sounds of chains rattling returned.

I yelled, thrusting my arm into the sky, dragging the flames with it.

Roaring like a wild beast, the fire shot into the air, chasing away the shadows and showing us how many goblins we faced. I counted ten sets of eyes lit up as the flames crashed to the ground, striking the goblins. They bellowed their war cries and charged the camp. Embers shot through the air, seeking out their intended targets as shields met brawn, and the fight ensued.

Trolian flipped a goblin over his shield, and a second broke past him, aiming right for me.

I raised my sword and dagger, catching his jagged blade, shoving him away. He roared, baring his sharpened teeth, and whaled on me. His attacks pushed me back until I managed to dig my boots in and regain a steady footing. I bashed in his knee with a hard kick and slashed along his thigh to his hip. He grunted and staggered forward.

I used his momentum to drive him to the ground and ran him through. His body shuddered then went limp. There was hardly time to catch my breath when a second goblin crashed into my back.

I rolled to my feet in time to get slashed in the arm. I ducked under his wide swing and went in low, cutting at his side with my blades. He sank to his knees, and I charged around him.

The goblins kept coming, and I lost myself in the fight. I expected them to be Red Wolf goblins, but the brand on my latest victim's arm was of the Bloodied Fist. The scouts had sworn there were no camps on the path we had taken, and yet here was an entire war party out for blood.

I swung around to see Nienna clutching her sword, her gaze fixated on the battle. The goblins' numbers dwindled, and soon there were only a few left. I latched onto the back of one trying to stab Trolian and relieved him of his head. The elves chased off a few more until there were only two left standing. I sheathed my dagger and was about to tell Trolian we should send the warriors out, just in case, when Nienna shouted.

"Alred!"

I whipped around to find her with her sword aimed at a goblin. He was severely wound, his black blood dripping from the wounds in his side. He held one hand to the injuries and offered his other up in surrender.

"Don't kill me," he grunted to Nienna. "Please. Let me go."

Nienna's hands shook, her eyes fixed on the goblin at the end of her sword. Part of me said to finish him off and save her the trouble of making this decision, but she had to face this choice on her own.

Trolian waved the elves to surround the two of them. The goblin continued to plead for his life.

I watched the struggle in Nienna's eyes and

knew the second she made up her mind. She lowered her sword and backed away.

"Go," she whispered.

The goblin lowered his head. His hand reached for a dagger that had fallen to the ground.

I bellowed, rushing forward to attack him, but Nienna beat me to it. She dodged the first swipe of the dagger and swung the sword, slashing through the goblin's throat. He gurgled, choking on his blood, the rest spraying from the wound at his throat. The dagger hit the ground, and he landed beside it, bleeding out in seconds.

Nienna stumbled back, the sword falling from her hands. Blood covered her front, and she wiped at it, face scrunching in panic.

I rushed to her side, taking hold of her face. "Nienna, look at me."

She kept shaking her head and whispering, "No," over and over.

"Nienna."

Her gaze locked onto mine, and she froze. "Alred. What, what did I just do?"

"You did what you had to do." I smoothed her hair from her face, my brow furrowing. "Come on, let's get you cleaned up."

I guided her to her tent and away from the dead

goblins littering our camp. I shoved the canvas aside and sat her down on her cot. I lit more candles from our supply stash and, using a cloth near the washbasin, set to work on removing the blood from her face and neck. She said nothing the entire time I worked, scrubbing her hands until they were clean, and checked over the rest of her quickly. There was blood in her hair, and I worked it out the best I could.

"Jurgis packed an extra set of clothes for you," I told her. "I'll lay them out, and you can change."

She nodded but didn't look at me.

"Nienna," I tried again, crouching in front of her. "If you hadn't killed him, he would've killed you. You did the right thing." I squeezed her hands, praying for some kind of reaction.

All she did was sit and stare.

I sighed, found the fresh clothes, and laid them on the cot. As I turned to go, she snatched my arm, digging her nails in hard enough to make me wince.

"This is how it starts," she said on a breath.

"How what starts?" I knelt on the ground, studying her carefully. "Nienna? Talk to me."

"I'll lose myself. I'll disappear, and it's all because of this night. I know it."

"You're not going to disappear." What was she

even talking about? "Does this have anything to do with what you saw?"

She squeezed my arm harder, and I covered her hand with mine. "I saw a battle. There were dead elves on the ground, and goblins were everywhere." She gulped, and it took a few tries for her to get the next words out. "I saw us."

"Us? There fighting?"

"We were surrounded. There was no way we were going to win, but the *me* in the vision, she wasn't me. She was someone dark and vicious. She was cold. The way she cut down those goblins, that isn't me. That fury can't really be inside me, can it?"

The notion that she had a vision of us that seemed far into the future worried me almost more than what she had seen herself turn into. "War changes people," I finally said. "It twists us. Sometimes for the better and sometimes not."

"I don't want to lose myself here."

"You won't," I promised. "Nienna, look at me."

It took a few seconds, but those dark green eyes found mine. The fear for what the future would bring screamed at me from those depths and stole whatever words I'd been about to tell her. She was a good person, an innocent. I said I'd never lie to her, and I wasn't going to start now. The person she was would have to adapt to survive in Kenzu'grote. She would have to find that inner strength and find ways not to lose herself as every Historian before her had found. But in the end, even Garrick had started to lose his will to show mercy to the enemy. His eyes had slowly turned cold after he returned Millie to the human world. I thought of the only thing I could say that wasn't a lie.

"I want you to hold on to the kindness in you, the good in your heart. You hold on to it and remind yourself every day that's why you're fighting. So others like you, other innocents, can have a chance to live in a world without war, and hopefully, the war will end before that vision comes true."

"I don't know if I can," she admitted.

"You have to try. You're a hell of a lot stronger than you think you are. One day, you'll realize you're not the pushover you let everyone think you are."

Tears shimmered in her eyes, and the next moment, she was in my arms. The shock at having her clinging to me made me slow to wrap my arms around her, holding her close as we sat on the ground in her tent. She was so small. I rested my cheek atop her head, soothing her with whatever words came to mind. The elvish words seemed to calm her down, and I ran my hand through her hair until she sniffed and lifted her head. She flattened her hands to my chest, her eyes searching mine.

I drew her in, my heart pounding. Just as I had back in the garden, I sensed her pain and fear. They pulled me to her, and gently, I brushed my lips against hers. A voice in the back of my mind said to remember my oath, but she whispered my name, and I told my worries to eff off.

I crushed her to me. She fisted her hands in my shirt, kissing me fiercely. The reason she was here, why I was, the fighting, everything disappeared until it was just Nienna in my arms and her lips to mine.

I deepened the kiss. I couldn't remember the last time I'd been this close to another person. What we were doing struck me full in the chest. She just killed her first goblin and was coming to grips with who and what she was.

Reluctantly, I pulled back. "We can talk more about this in the morning. I should let you get some rest," I murmured lamely, the ache in my chest turning to a hollow pang as she tried to hide her disappointment.

"Oh, uh, okay, if that's what you want."

It wasn't what I wanted, not even close, but it's

what I had to do. We stood, and with my neck on fire, I rushed out of her tent. She called after me, but I kept walking until I was at the edge of the camp. What had I been thinking? I couldn't get involved with her. Not only was I her Protector, but I knew exactly how this relationship would end. It would be the same as the rest of them ended—in pain and heartbreak. No good would come of us being together. None.

"It's the bond," I muttered to myself. "It's just ramping up your emotions. That's all this is. What you're feeling isn't real. You'll get over it, you both will." Adrenaline and the bond, that's what drove me to kiss her. It didn't matter how much I was drawn to her or how attractive she was.

A relationship with the Historian could not happen. End of story.

"Alred? Is Nienna alright?" Trolian asked, appearing at my side.

"She's shaken up, but she's fine," I reported. "Are the goblins taken care of?"

"Yes, and we found two of our own wounded but alive. Even one death is still too much to bear." He whispered a quick blessing for the dead elf then gave me a quizzical look. "What happened in that tent?"

"Nothing."

"Doesn't look like nothing."

"It is," I snapped. "I'm going to get some sleep. Wake me when it's my turn for the watch."

Trolian caught my arm when I went to walk away. "You're allowed to be happy, you know."

"You've been talking to Jurgis too much."

"Maybe, but he's right. I see how you look at her; we all do."

"And? I have a calling to uphold as does she."

Trolian sighed, releasing my arm. "Last I heard, there's no rule saying you can't be with the Historian. Just saying. Don't fight what you're feeling, especially if the war's about to get worse. You won't get a second chance."

I stalked through the camp and took up my post just outside Nienna's tent. I almost walked right back inside, but forced myself to sit on the ground instead. What confused me more than my actions were hers.

She'd kissed me back.

There'd been no hesitation in her touch at all.

I lay back, listening to the quiet murmur of the warriors and wondered what she was going to tell Phil once we rescued him.

Chapter 10
NIENNA

Taking down my tent and helping pack up camp, my mind replayed the kiss with Alred. My attraction to him wasn't what shocked me. It was how he'd kissed me while he held me in his arms. The explosion of emotions from him shot right through me, and I wanted to cling to him the rest of the night.

Then something seemed to click in his mind, as if he realized what we were doing, and it was over. After he'd left my tent, I changed into fresh clothes and fell onto my cot, wishing he'd come back. I'd been terrified of falling asleep and seeing my sword cutting into that goblin. When I closed my eyes, though, it was Alred I dreamt about. When I woke this morning, hearing him calling out orders to the elves. I remembered vividly what happened last night.

"Too bad, it'll probably be a one-time thing," I mumbled, shoving the tent canvas roughly into the leather satchel. "Leave it to him to make me even more confused than I already am about everything."

The last twenty-four hours had me completely twisted around. I was learning how to fight while tracking down a band of goblins who'd stolen Phil and a sacred tome. And the elf who was pushing me and pushing me to get over my doubts, the one person I thought might not care for me, went out of his way to comfort me and kissed me like we were both trying to save each other from drowning.

When he'd ended the kiss, his furrowed brow told me he was confused, too.

Then he'd left.

Sometimes I really, really hated men.

"Nienna?"

I shot upright to find Alred watching me, his lip twitching as if he was trying not to smile. "Hey, uh, almost packed up."

"You're fine. I wanted to talk to you before we set out."

"About last night? I'm okay. I mean, I'm not exactly over the whole I killed something thing, and now I'm terrified I'm still going to turn into some messed up version of myself. But I'm keeping it together. No worries here."

He blinked at me. His neck turned red, and he grunted. "Right. I'm glad to hear it. I was actually coming over to apologize for my actions."

My heart sank. "Oh."

"I'm not sure what came over me, and it was highly inappropriate for me to do that while you're with Phil, and I'm sorry. I shouldn't have put you in that situation."

"Right, Phil. Uh, about that. I broke up with him."

Alred crossed his arms over his chest. "You did? When?"

"Actually, it's been a long time coming, but yeah, the day everything went sideways, I ended it. You don't have to worry about putting me in an awkward situation."

"That's uh, that's good then." He coughed.

I smirked, enjoying seeing the stoic, bossy Alred nervous for once. "Are you still sorry for kissing me?"

His gaze dipped to my lips, and he sighed.

"Sorry for it? No, but I fear it's not something we should not have a repeat of."

"Why?"

"Various reasons."

"Probably boring and pointless reasons," I mumbled. "This have to do with who we are to each other?"

"Yes, if I'm honest. Our priorities must be to our callings."

"And you think we can't do that if we're in a relationship?"

He squared his shoulders, nodding. "The only thing we need to be worrying about right now is getting Phil and the tome back. Anything else can wait."

Jurgis was right. Alred closed his emotions off from me right before my eyes. His face took on that careful blank expression. The only thing he couldn't hide was the way the gold flecks flared brightly when he looked at me. That kiss meant something last night. No matter what Alred claimed, he felt something in those few moments. If I was going to be stuck in this world with a threat of death hanging over me, I wasn't about to pretend there were no sparks flying between us. I'd leave it alone until we were back in Vel'Baram.

"So, what you did last night with the fire," I said, catching his thankful glance, "how did you do that?"

"Magic, the same I used to put you to sleep."

"Can I do stuff like that?"

"I'm not sure. Garrick wasn't able to use magic, but there's always a chance for you."

"Probably best I can't," I said, finished packing up the leather bag, and hoisted it onto my back. The rest of the elves were ready to move out, and we set forth together. The two who were too wounded to go on stayed behind with three to watch over them until they were healed enough to make it back to Vel'Baram. "Why don't you use it more? Your magic, I mean," I asked as we walked.

"Tapping into the pulse of magic takes its toll. In the human world, more so than here, but it still costs energy. Weakens the user. If I relied solely on magic, I'd be out of a fight in ten minutes, maybe less," he explained.

"That fast?"

"Yes. The gods granted us the ability to use magic to assist us in our lives, not to rely on it. It's why I tend to avoid it."

"You are pretty handy with a sword," I agreed, loving when he smirked. "Watching you fight is insane. The way you move, it's like you're not even thinking. You just go with it."

"Instinct, as I've told you. Once you learn to let it take over, you'll be able to fight like that, too."

The vision of my future self flashed through my mind. "Yeah, sure I will."

Trolian called Alred's name, and he picked up the pace to catch up to the captain, leaving another elf to take his place with me. I walked in silence, contemplating what these next days and weeks would bring me. Alred told me to hold onto who I was now, but also that I had to adapt. I had to become stronger. I couldn't let fear keep weighing me down. If I was going to survive, I had to learn to fight. I waited for a burst of understanding to hit me and chase away my doubts, but nothing happened. There was no epiphany moment. No realizing deep down, this was where I was supposed to be.

I merely felt torn and alone.

Alred would never understand what I was going through. Maybe he was right, and we shouldn't pursue a relationship. I huffed to myself, waving away the warrior's curious glance.

I'd hoped that by coming on this journey to save

Phil the last missing pieces of my destiny, and all that nonsense would fall into place. I was left with more questions than answers and had no idea how I was going to pick up where dear old Dad left off. This was hopeless.

***

I crouched beside Alred, using what little brush there was as cover. One of the scouts had come to find us about an hour ago saying the goblins had made camp for the night, and they had a human with them. We left our gear behind and followed the scout along a narrow path that ran beside a sludge-filled river. The stench made me gag. Even farther away, the smell continued to waft across my face.

"Only eight," Trolian whispered to Alred, sinking down beside him.

"And Phil? Did you see him?"

"He's tied up. Beaten but alive. If they have the tome, I can't see it."

Guilt made my chest tight, hearing Phil had been hurt. Everything he'd gone through these last few days was on me. So much for protecting the innocent. I had to make this right. Everyone wanted me to be the hero, and it looked like Phil was going to be the first person I saved. Not sure if they'd listen or not, I prayed to whatever gods might be listening to not let me chicken out. I could do this. I would do this. I was the damned Historian.

I peered through the dense, dead shrubs trying to get a glimpse of Phil.

Alred dragged me back, scowling.

"What? We can't let them kill Phil."

"We won't, but you are not going to move from this spot."

"They want me," I argued quietly. "I should be the one to go in. I can be bait."

Alred's eyes narrowed, and his hand closed around my wrist. "Have you lost it?"

"What? I can distract them, and you guys can do your badassery, kill them, and we can get the tome, save Phil, and hurry out of there. Right? Sounds like a plan to me."

"A horrible plan," Alred replied.

"She has a point, though."

Alred glared daggers at Trolian. "Come again?"

"They want her alive. They won't harm her. It'll give us time to get into position."

"See? The captain agrees with me."

Alred muttered in elvish. I was fairly sure he was cursing out Trolian and me. "I can't just sit back and let the Historian wander into a goblin camp."

"Look, I dragged Phil into this shit," I reminded him. "I have to fix it."

"And you will be doing as I say."

A voice whispered through my mind that I knew what I had to do. Alred wanted me to stop doubting myself, this would be a start. Unless I got myself killed, then hey, at least I wouldn't be killed by a book.

Not sure what drove me to act, I tugged on Alred's collar and kissed him. He stilled for a second. When his lips moved against mine, I pressed myself into him.

"For luck," I whispered, stood, and ran out of our hiding spot before he could stop me.

He whispered my name harshly, but it was too late.

I walked toward the goblin camp, shaking out my hands and doing my best to not let my knees give out from the sudden fear swarming me. What the hell had I been thinking? This was a terrible, horrible idea. The goblins hadn't seen me yet, and I considered sneaking back to Alred.

A pained moan came from the other side of the

campfire, and I spotted Phil lying on his side, hands bound behind his back, and a gag shoved in his mouth. His right eye was swollen shut and bruised, and dried blood covered the rest of his face and his shirt. His right arm rested at an odd angle.

Jurgis had said to use my fear, shape it into something else. I wasn't simply afraid of those goblins; I was pissed at what they did to someone I cared about. Bit by bit, my fear turned into anger, and I pulled on it, willing it to give me strength.

As I was debating what to do next with my brilliant plan, a goblin with a fur cloak chucked another log onto the fire. "They should've been here by now."

"You know the Bloodied Fist. They don't keep to anyone's schedule but their own," a second goblin snarled.

"Don't know why we need to wait for them. We're the ones that captured the human. We set the trap. It should be our clan that gets the glory, not theirs."

"But we will. You heard what the leaders said."

Their conversation died off, and the cloaked goblin grunted, spitting into the fire. The Bloodied First. Those were the goblins who attacked us. Calling on all the stories Mom told me of Garrick, the hero, I told myself that's all this was, another story. Only this time, I was playing the role of the hero.

Squaring my shoulders, I took another step forward, put my fingers to my lips, and whistled.

Eight goblins jerked their heads in my direction, four of them jumping to their feet.

"Evening, assholes," I said, planting a smile on my face in hopes my act of bravado would hide my unease. "I'll be taking that human with me now if you don't mind."

The goblins exchanged looks then cackled. The tallest one with the fur cloak came forward, his massive weathered hand resting on the hilt of a wickedly sharp looking dagger. "Is that so?" He sniffed the air and snarled. "Half breed."

"Good job," I mocked, giving him a thumb's up. "I'm also the Historian."

The goblin's dark eyes narrowed. "You?"

"Yeah, me. Got a problem with that?" The goblin took another step closer, and I staggered back, unable to keep holding onto my fearless façade. "You going to hand him over or not?" I demanded.

"I'm afraid we have other orders." The goblin snapped his fingers, and the seven with him spread out, blocking my view of Phil. I thought I heard him try to say my name. "You're going to come with us nice and quiet now."

I took another step back, wondering what was taking Alred so damned long. "Yeah, that's not going to happen and if you try to take me, you'll regret it."

The goblin's narrow eyebrow arched, an amused grin stretching his cracked and dried lips. "That so? What are you going to do? Talk us to death?"

I planted my hands on my hips, shrugging. "No, but I think I'll slaughter you like I did those other goblins. Blooded Fist members, I think they were. Shame, really. Now they're all dead because they came after me. So," I said, clapping my hands, "how about we make a deal? Hand over the human and my tome, and I'll let you all live. Sounds fair."

A few of the goblins gave me uncertain looks, but their leader wasn't so easy to convince. He scratched at his chin, then burst out in laughter. "You lie."

"I'm far more powerful than I look." I held up my hand and, crossing the fingers of my other hand, in hope Alred was paying attention. I snapped my fingers, and the fire cracked sharply. I gave a slight nod of approval since I'd had no way of knowing if Alred was going to figure out what to do.

The goblins jumped, and I hid my sigh of relief. Embers burst from the center of the fire, shooting out into the night. They landed on the goblins' arms, making them hop around, hurrying to put them out.

"Are we going to make a deal or not?"

The leader grabbed the dagger from his belt and held it at the ready, stalking closer. "Oh, we're going to make a deal, my sweet half breed, but I don't think you're going to like it much."

The last shred of my courage faltered, and I opened my mouth to scream for Alred when a dagger thunked into the goblin's forehead. He fell to his knees, his eyes crossing, staring up at the hilt protruding from his head. The rest of the goblins drew their swords, and the elves shouted, charging into camp.

Alred rushed past me and took hold of my hand.

"Get Phil," he ordered. He placed his sword in my hand and urged me on as he joined the fight.

A weapon in hand, I ducked and weaved through the skirmish, skidding in the dry dirt to

Phil's side. I sat him up and worked at untying the ropes binding him while he peered at me with his one good eye. A dirty rag had been tied around his mouth, and I shoved that down, giving him a chance to breathe easier.

"Nienna," he gasped. "What the hell is this?"

"Questions later," I muttered, working furiously at the ropes, while the fight carried on around us. "We have to get you out of here. The tome. Where is it?"

He nodded toward a stone by the fire. "One of their bags."

The ropes continued to fray, and he was nearly free when he shouted in warning. I spotted the hulking shadow, shoved Phil to the side, and dove out of the way.

Alred yelled, and then he was there, raising another sword to block the goblin's attack. He kicked the beast back and plunged his sword into his chest. As the goblin died, Alred stood protectively over me, and I finished freeing Phil. He could hardly stand, and I threw his arm over my shoulders, ready to get the tome and make a run for it.

All but one goblin was dead, but after being attacked by the Bloodied Fist and what I'd overheard the goblins saying, I wasn't sure sticking around was a good idea.

"Did you hear them?" I asked Alred as he took up Phil's other arm.

"I did. We can't stay."

"Wait, this guy? Weren't you on campus?" Phil murmured to Alred.

"Save your energy," Alred told him sternly. "It's a long trek to safety."

"Where the hell are we? And those things—are those goblins?"

Alred grunted.

We reached the area Phil pointed out to me, and I dug through the leather satchels, searching for the tome. My hand hit something leathery, and I tugged out the tome with a triumphant shout. I'd barely picked it up when my body froze, and a tugging started in my gut.

"Nienna," Alred said, reaching for me.

My vision blurred, and the next thing I knew, I stood in the Archives. I blinked, spinning around, trying to figure out how I managed to get here. Torches burst to life along the walls, all the way to the ceiling, and the gold-lettered covers on the tomes shimmered in the flickering light.

"Nienna, at long last."

Clenching my jaw, I turned to find the elf from the painting, smiling sadly down at me. The man Mom talked about for years as the hero in all her stories. The elf she loved. "Garrick?"

He started to lift his hand, but let it fall. "I'm so sorry I didn't come to you sooner. I'm sorry for a lot of things I did wrong as a father. I don't expect you to forgive me, but—"

I rushed to him and embraced him, cutting off his apology. Tears slipped from my eyes when he wrapped his arms around me and held me the only way a dad could.

I wanted to hate him, but after everything I'd just been through, what Mom endured for the love of this elf, my grudge disappeared under his proud gaze.

"I never meant for you to follow my path," he whispered. "But I know you will fulfill your calling. You will be a great Historian and a hero just as I was."

"I'm not sure about the hero part."

He sighed, glancing around the Archives. "I wasn't sure I could do it either, in the beginning. The world was in chaos, and everyone looked to me to set it right. It's not fair to have this burden fall on your shoulders, but you must remember, you are not alone. You have me and the rest of us here with you always. And you have Alred." His lip twitched, and my cheeks grew hot. "I think you're going to be good for him."

"Are you trying to set up your daughter?"

"Maybe. Can you blame me?" He tucked my hair behind my ears, his eyes sad. "I missed so much with you. Gods, you look like your mom."

"She misses you."

His face crumpled, and he sucked in a harsh breath. "It killed me to send her to the human world, but I had no choice."

"I know, Dad. I know."

His eyes crinkled at my words. "Dad. I haven't heard you say that since you were a toddler."

"Those weren't dreams?"

"No, no, they were not." He hugged me again, kissing the top of my head. When he set me back on my feet, his face was serious. "I hoped to be further along with fixing the damage done by the goblins, but sadly, my time came much too soon. You need to find a way to finish what I started. Bring an end to the war where I couldn't."

"I'm not like you," I argued.

"Nor do I expect you to be. You will find a way

to be the Historian in your own way, just as I did. Just as every Historian before you has."

"Alred's teaching me to fight."

"As he should. This world is dangerous," Garrick said, his eyes darkening. "Your mother paid the price for my arrogance. Listen to Alred. Learn everything you can from him, and you'll survive."

"Until the book decides it's my turn to die."

He cupped my cheek. "Sometimes, heroes must make sacrifices for the greater good. One day, you might have to do the same, but there's always a chance you won't. It's not an easy life to accept, but someone has to do the job."

"And if it changes me into someone I don't recognize?"

He frowned.

I told him of the vision I had of Alred and me, one that couldn't have been of any time soon. "Did you ever see something that far in the future?"

"I didn't, but the tome speaks to each of us differently. If it's showing you this moment, then it's important."

Panic fluttered in my gut until Garrick rested his hands on my shoulders.

"You can do this, Nienna. Do not doubt yourself, not anymore. Fear is a part of life. Use it, grow stronger, and save Kenzu'grote. Tell Alred he was a true friend and make sure he knows he didn't fail me." Tears shone in his eyes, his body fading from sight. "I'm proud of you, my daughter. So proud."

"Dad, wait," I yelled, but he vanished. "Dad!"

The Archives swirled around me, and I was swarmed by images all over again. Somehow, I knew I was seeing from the very beginning of the war all the way to the present day. There was so much bloodshed and death, so many crying out for help it tore me apart. I had to do something to stop their agony. Voices whispered in my ears, but they were too low and twisted to understand. The images faded, and my eyes fluttered open.

Wooden beams crossed over my head. Warm sunlight poured into the room, confusing me even more. I was lying in bed, the same one in Garrick's old chamber. How had I gotten here?

"Nienna?"

I turned my head to find a familiar face. "Alred? Where are we? What happened?"

He was at my side in an instant, holding my hand. "You gave me a heart attack is what you did. Never, ever use yourself as bait again, understand?" he ordered. "Never again."

I smiled, squeezing his hand. "Can't make any promises."

He shook his head and leaned over me, kissing my forehead. The sweet action had my breath catching, and when he sat back, his face was flushed. Roughly, he muttered something in elvish then released my hand. I wanted his warmth back, but he moved to the foot of my bed, pacing.

"We're back in Vel'Baram," he told me. "After you touched the tome, you fainted, and we couldn't rouse you. You've been asleep for a week."

"A week? Did the rest of the elves make it back okay? And Phil?"

"Those wounded are healing, including Phil," he assured me. "And, the tome is here." He pointed to the desk by the windows.

I threw my shaky legs over the side of the bed, noting the fluttery blue sleeveless nightgown I was in and wondering where it came from. I went to the desk, but when I moved my hand toward the tome, Alred was there to stop me. He caught my wrist, dragging me away from the desk and right into his hard chest.

"No, I'll not watch you collapse again."

"I won't."

"How do you know?" he asked, not letting me go.

"I saw what I needed to see. I talked to Garrick, and I was shown the full history of the war. I guess covering a couple of thousand years of history will knock you on your ass for a week," I commented lightly, Alred's brow furrowed more. "Hey, I'm fine, see? Just feel kind of weak."

He grunted in reply, his chest rising and falling in time with mine. "You should get some more rest."

"Whatever you say, bossy pants."

His eyes narrowed, but I tugged on his shirt and pulled him down to me. I kissed him softly, smiling when he gave in with another grunt and held me in his arms. He lifted me off my feet, the room growing exceedingly hot as he left me breathless. But just like the first time, he drew back too damned soon and put some space between us.

"We can't do this," he whispered harshly. "I'm sorry. Get some rest."

"Alred," I called when he was at the door, "Garrick wanted me to tell you something."

He gripped the door handle, not turning back around. "I don't need to hear his curses."

"Actually, he said to remind you that you were a

true friend and that you didn't fail him." I considered mentioning Garrick hoped we would somehow hit it off, but that was a conversation for another day. "Alred?"

He nodded. "Thank you for telling me. Sleep, Nienna, I'll send Jurgis to check on you soon."

Then he was gone.

I tapped my fingers on the cover of Garrick's tome. I still had no idea what I was doing, not really, but I no longer felt alone. I had the spirits of the Historians with me, as Garrick said. And I had Alred. Lips tingling from our kiss, I smiled to myself and made my way back to bed, yawning as I fell to the mattress. I'd just have to prove to Alred that no matter what dangers Kenzu'grote and the goblins threw at us, we could face them together and come out the other side alive.

For how long? the doubting voice whispered. *You saw that future. You saw there was no escape. And besides, if that fight doesn't kill you, the tome will. Do you really want to put him through that much heartache? He'll have to watch you die, and he'll blame himself. Forever.*

My eyes shot open, and I fisted my hands in the blankets, trying to shut out the voice. But maybe it was right. Could I do that to Alred? Could I leave him heartbroken? He deserved some happiness in his life, but being with me meant he'd lose me in the end. Throwing my arm over my eyes, I decided one way or another, I'd make sure Alred got his happy ending, even if it wasn't with me.

That was my job, after all. I was destined to save everyone in Kenzu'grote, and that included Alred.

"This is going to suck," I mumbled, rolled over, and tried to get some sleep.

____

Chapter 11
ALRED

____

The ceremony for Garrick took place when the suns set over Vel'Baram. Their rays lit up the courtyard filled with elves gathered to say their goodbyes. His body had been preserved until the time was right to send him on. I was dressed in black, along with everyone here. Tears slipped down Nienna's cheeks while flowers and herbs were placed around Garrick's body on the pyre.

I had told her before the ceremony she would be asked to light the fire to send Garrick on. With a soft smile, she'd rested her hand on my arm and said I should be the one to do it.

Now, as Thalia brought the silver-handled torch to me, I hesitated. Nienna gave me an encouraging smile, even through her tears. I took the torch and walked to the pyre. I had yet to stop to let myself grieve for the death of my friend. I rested the flames to the wood, watched them catch fire, and couldn't stop the pain from engulfing me. I tried to keep them back, but a few tears escaped my control.

"I'll miss you, old friend," I whispered as the flames surrounded Garrick's body in a cocoon. "But I swear to you I will not fail your daughter. I will keep her safe, no matter the cost to my life."

I bowed and backed away. One by one, the elves walked to the pyre and bowed before moving on. Nienna spoke quietly with Jurgis, their hands clasped together as if they were already good friends. It wouldn't surprise me. They were both innocents in a world filled with darkness and death.

She caught my eye, and I subtly bowed then walked away, needing space to think.

I hadn't slept well since returning to Vel'Baram with an unconscious Nienna in my arms. Watching her collapse at the goblin camp had stirred up fierce emotions I'd never thought I'd experience in my lifetime. Fear of losing her had crushed my chest and left my stomach in painful knots. The loneliness she'd managed to chase away these last few days flooded back tenfold. I stayed with her every hour of every day until she finally opened her eyes.

Then she'd kissed me, and I'd forgotten I told her we needed to keep our distance. I paced madly through the corridors with my head lowered while I talked myself out of being with Nienna.

I told myself it was the heat of the moment. That's all those kisses were. These feelings I had for her, I'd honestly never be able to tell if they were real or simply from the bond we shared.

That's a lie, my subconscious whispered. *It's been real with her since the second you saw her.*

"I can't be with her," I'd argued with myself quietly. "I know how this ends."

Do you? Or are you scared to feel something real?

My boots came to a harsh stop on the stone floor. I was never scared of anything.

"Alred, do you have a moment?" Thalia had called from behind me.

Making sure my face concealed my warring emotions, I turned. "Of course."

"I know this is your time to mourn, but we have yet to speak about what you overheard at the goblin camp. Trolian told us, but I wanted to hear your thoughts," she said.

"I agree with Trolian. It sounds as if the Bloodied Fist are attempting to gain control of the clans."

"You think he can do it? Ioc?"

"He's a manipulative bastard. His clan's the reason the war began in the first place. But I'm not sure it's him we need to worry about. Ioc is old for a goblin. His sons, however, those twins are the ones we should concern ourselves with."

Ioc might have figured out how to use the Historian against us, but it was his sons, Brink and Bracken I worried about more. Ioc was cold and calculated. The twins were vicious. All they wanted was more bloodshed. For the last decade, they'd been the ones leading the charge into battle. If they managed to gain complete control over the clans, become their kings, the vision Nienna told me of would come true. We would lose this war. The last I heard, they already had quite the backing from many in their own clan. The second Ioc died, we'd be fighting every day to hold them back.

"The tides of war are changing," I told Thalia. "I fear for the coming days."

"As do we all." She glanced down the hall in the direction of the Archives. "We have our Historian.

She will see us through this as they have always done."

I imagined Nienna wading into battle as Garrick had done and fisted my hands, fighting back a stream of curses. "I'm sure she will."

A day after Nienna had awakened, she was taken to the Seven once again and presented with Garrick's tome. Without hesitation, she accepted her calling. Her father's book disappeared from her hands to take its place in the Archives as a new, empty tome took its place in her hands. The bond between us was sealed at that moment. She'd turned to me, smiling, but there was a sadness in her eyes I didn't understand. I thought it was for Garrick, but my gut said it was for someone else.

"I will leave you to your mourning," Thalia said, pulling me from my thoughts.

"There is one more thing," I said, keeping her there. "Before Garrick's death, he told me you needed to see the final page he wrote."

"What did it say?"

"I have not had a chance to read it."

"I'll check the tome and share the news with the others."

I nodded, and she walked away, leaving me to continue wandering the halls.

Tonight, I would mourn because tomorrow Nienna's real training began. Maybe if I pushed her, made her hate me, ignoring my need to be with her would far easier. She had seen through that act the first time. I doubted I'd be able to pull it off. Cursing, I stormed to my chambers, slammed the door shut, and decided drinking alone the rest of the night was a perfect plan.

* * *

Nienna hugged Phil, but whatever she was saying to him, I was too far away to hear. He'd spent the last few days in Vel'Baram healing from his wounds. The goblins had done a number on him, physically and mentally. Trolian was tasked with returning the human to his world safely. There was one last task to be completed before he could leave, however.

I watched Nienna's face when she took the small vial from Thalia. She turned back to Phil and offered it to him. The shimmering gold liquid inside was familiar. It was the same potion given to Millie to make her forget the torture and torment the goblins put her through. Her love for Garrick had fought against the potion, but we were confident it would work on Phil. That he wouldn't have the same struggle Millie had.

This morning, Thalia told Nienna it would be best for her ex-boyfriend if he didn't remember being here and if he didn't remember her. She'd argued at first, but later came to realize it was for the best.

Phil's eyes glazed over, and a calm smile spread across his face as the potion took effect.

Nienna backed away, and Trolian led Phil through the gardens and out the gate. He had another vial to give to Alice, Nienna's other friend. That had been her suggestion. She didn't want her friend spending years searching for her if she was never going home.

I had yet to share with her the latest news, or rather lack of. Thalia had found me this morning to let me know she checked Garrick's tome to find the final pages had been torn free. Whatever Garrick had seen moments before his death was now in the hands of the enemy. My gut told me it had to do with the goblin twins, but now we'd have to wait until Nienna had her first true vision.

"So," Nienna said, her bright tone clearly forced, "what's on the agenda for today?"

"Training, as will be every day."

"Sounds exciting." She picked at her nails, and I nearly reached over to stop her. "You think he'll be okay?"

"I do."

"And Mom?"

"Something tells me Garrick's spirit will find its way to her. Millie is strong. She'll endure."

Nienna bobbed her head and let out a heavy sigh. "Right, so, training. Is this Historian training or sword training?"

"Both," I said as we turned and walked down the stone path.

"Great, so I can get my ass kicked by you. Again."

It's how you learn."

"Sure, it is. You just enjoy seeing me get all pissed off."

I tilted my head. She did have a certain fiery beauty when she was yelling at me in aggravation, her cheeks red and her hair flying madly about her face. I glanced over to see her brow arched. "What?"

"Nothing. Just making plans of my own."

I stopped when she chuckled. "What does that mean? Nienna?"

"Come on! Are we training or what?" she replied.

"She's going to be a pain in my ass," I murmured, prayed for patience, then followed her, something I felt I was going to be doing a lot of soon enough.

The Tome
THE GOBLIN ARCHIVES BOOK TWO

Nienna's not a librarian in Portland Oregon. Nope. Not anymore. She's now in another world serving as a Historian to a population of elves. She's obligated to a life of recording her visions in a tome. A tome which seems to be hellbent on recording her death and Alred's heartbreak.

Alred Lightvale. Elf. Hot. Protector of the Historian. He's fallen in love with the Historian but he doesn't understand why she won't let him in. She's trying to keep a dark secret from him and he's hellbent on keeping her alive. And in his life. No matter what dark entity is trying to destroy their world.

Chapter 1

NIENNA

Goblins swarmed me, and I raised my sword, striking out at anything that came too close. There were too many. We weren't going to make it.

I spotted Alred through the mass of bodies, but no other elves caught my eye. We were the only ones left on the battlefield. He cut a bloody path to me, and we pressed our backs to each other.

Alred threw a look over his shoulder, the gold flecks in his eyes flaring to life with fury and regret. There was no more time for words. Goblins surged forward. The trees burned as the fire spread, consuming everything in its path. Flames tore across the field and straight for us.

Alred grabbed hold of my free hand, squeezing

it tightly as we faced our end together. Just as the flames reached out to swallow us, I screamed—

My eyes shot open, and I wildly glanced around the room. I sank to the bed in a heap, panting for air. I was safe, back in Vel'Baram. There was no fire and no great battle with the goblins, not yet, at least. I was safe, and so was Alred. We were alive.

We still had time.

Cold sweat covered my forehead, and annoyed, I wiped it away with my hand. It'd been nearly five weeks since Phil went back home and was made to forget about me. I missed him, Alice, and Mom, but there was no going back. The call to being the Historian was in full swing, including never-ending training with Alred, Jurgis, and Thalia.

I glanced out the window and found the suns weren't even peeking over the horizon yet. Leaves fluttered past my window in the crisp morning air, and I shivered, pulling the quilts up higher around my shoulders. Thalia had told me the seasons were changing quickly. She hadn't been kidding. A few days ago, it had been hot. Now, the leaves rapidly faded from yellows and greens to oranges and reds, and the nights were cold, leaving behind a thin layer of frost.

The sight of the landscape turning from

summer to fall was breathtaking. I'd grown used to it and felt more at home with it each passing day. It probably helped I was in Dad's old rooms. Garrick Havard, my father, the last Historian and the man I grew up hearing about as a character in fairy tales told by Mom. A huge part of me doubted I'd be able to live up to his reputation, something Alred continued to lecture me on. To stop doubting myself. Some days, that elf knew how to push my buttons.

The last images of the nightmare came back to me while I pictured Alred's face. I stilled. That fire in that vision wasn't normal. It couldn't be. The flames moved as if they were alive. I overheard the Seven, Alred, and the Generals discussing what the goblins had been up to the last few months and their fear at what dark magic they were willing to unleash. That fire, it had to be part of their plans. But the vision still felt so far away, and it wasn't the only one I'd had. There had been one nearly every day, but all of them took place in the distant future. I hadn't told Alred, but sometimes, the images were fuzzy, like the scenes played out through a fog. They'd shift and change midway through, and I was left confused and out of sorts. Other times they were real, far too real, and I'd come out of the vision expecting to be dead.

I climbed out of bed, shivering when my bare feet hit the cold stone floor of my room. The long sweater-like robe I was given, as part of a new wardrobe, hung on the back of the wooden chair at the desk. I slipped into it quickly, tugging it around me, and rushed to find my slippers. My morning routine had gone from climbing out of bed, grabbing coffee, my books for class, and heading out the door, to stoking a fire in the hearth and dressing in clothes I never imagined I'd wear.

"At least there's indoor plumbing," I mused to myself with a laugh after I'd taken care of business.

I was getting better at building my own fires, too, mostly because I grew tired of having random elves show up in my room to do it for me. They'd appear without my even asking for help. It was one of the few small things I was proud of.

The other was that I managed to set up Alred on three random dates since I made my plan to ensure he found a way to be happy. The latest one had been last night. According to Jurgis, Cellica, a healer, had her eyes set on Alred for years, but he never noticed. I'd met her a few times, seeing as she lived in Vel'Baram and studied in the Central

Tower with Jurgis. She seemed friendly enough and pleasant to be around.

So, last night when Alred headed to the tavern, I made sure to let Cellica know he would be there and that he would love it if she would offer to buy him a drink, maybe dance for a bit.

Jurgis was the only other elf wise to my plan, and he thought it was great. I brushed out my hair, hoping that maybe Cellica would finally be the one to make that damned protector of mine smile.

My hands stilled, and I glanced at my reflection, a white-hot spike of jealousy I hadn't expected shot through me. "You're not jealous. You can't be. You're doing this for him. He said you couldn't be together, and you don't want to be anyway, because that freaking tome over there is going to kill you. Stick to the plan. Besides, not like he's tried to kiss you since that night."

The five weeks had been long, and each day, I'd waited to see if he would say anything about the heated moment we'd shared in my room. After the first three weeks, I stopped waiting and decided it was time to put my plan into action and find him someone to care for that wasn't me.

I swallowed back my longing for a relationship with Alred that wasn't simply one between the

Historian and Protector. Forgetting how he held me and kissed me hadn't been easy. If I wasn't having nightmares about that terrible vision, I dreamt about his holding me.

With my hair drawn back in a tight braid, so it was out of the way for training, I dressed in my usual pants, blouse, and a leather corset. Once I tugged my boots on, I ran my fingers over the cover of the tome.

So far, I'd recorded nearly thirty visions, but each of them had been far different than what I'd read in the tomes of the past Historians. What they had seen had come to pass within the next few days, sometimes hours. But what I witnessed, the atrocities and slaughter I'd been forced to see, felt so far away. Dad had told me each Historian was shown things differently, but somehow I knew everything I'd been shown so far had nothing to do with the coming days or weeks. My visions were further out. No matter what Thalia or Alred or anyone else told me, the foreboding growing in the pit of stomach said this was a sign. A bad one. I'd overheard Alred telling Trolian the tides of war were changing. I couldn't shake the feeling that they weren't turning in the elves' favor.

The hall was empty, save for a few of the staff

setting out breakfast. I helped myself to fresh coffee. Four guards stood at their posts, unmoving, as they were every morning, afternoon, and night. I'd asked Jurgis one day if they really needed that many guards. A sad look had come over his face, and he told me the generals feared the goblins were going to start trying to assassinate the Seven. There'd been two attempts, but thanks to the increased numbers of soldiers in Vel'Baram, they didn't get beyond the garden gate.

Their presence should've made me feel safe instead of uneasy, but they were a reminder of the war Kenzu'grote had been in for centuries. And now all that pressure was on me to ensure it came to an end, preferably one where the elves weren't wiped out of existence.

Steam rose from the mug, warming my face. The heated ceramic chased away the chill from my hands, and my mind drifted to my nightmare. No, not a nightmare. A vision of an event that would come to pass. Just like all the others I'd had. The dull echo of screaming sounded in my ears. My eyes went in and out of focus. They were dying, all those people in my visions, they were dying, and I wasn't strong enough to save them. Their shouts competed with the howling goblins and the crackling of that fire, eating everything in its path. I tilted my head, thinking back over every vision I'd had. It wasn't only the battlefield I had seen those hungry flames rampaging through. How the hell had I missed it?

Nienna.

The voice whispered in my mind.

I stilled.

I'd heard it before, I knew I had, but where?

Soon, Nienna, very soon… I have great plans for you…

"Nienna."

I yelped.

The mug slipped from my fingers, crashed to the table, and shattered.

"Damn it," I muttered, grabbing a napkin to mop up the spilled coffee.

Alred frowned, helping me pick up the broken mug.

"Thanks for scaring me."

"Wasn't my intention," he replied. "What do I always tell you?"

I glanced around, searching for who else might've said my name. Shit, if I was going to start hearing voices, my life was about to become far more complicated.

I was merely tired, I told myself, that's all—tired and hearing things.

"Can we not start with the lessons this early? The sun's barely up. And why are you even awake?"

He shrugged as he poured us more coffee and sat on the other side of the table. "I was awake, figured I might as well get up." The gold in his eyes glimmered, and the way his jaw tensed said that was a lie. The dark circles around his eyes mirrored my own most days. He might've been awake, but something jarred him from his obviously not so restful sleep.

Meaning me and my nightmares. I was starting to hate this connection we had with each other. Or he had to me. It wasn't fair that anytime I was afraid or about to have a mental breakdown, he sensed it and came running. How was I supposed to find him a pretty elf to have a life with if he was tied to me so closely?

"Yeah, sure you were," I finally murmured.

"Why are you up? You loathe mornings."

I returned his shrug with one of my own. "Was just up. So, how was last night?"

"Last night?"

"Yeah. Jurgis said something about you and

Trolian going to the tavern. I don't know. I was curious if anything fun happened."

"You're acting weird," he said, and my brow arched. "Weirder than normal."

"What? I can't ask you how your night was?"

"You can if you tell me why you're awake."

I squeezed my mug, thankful when more people meandered into the hall, as the Central Tower, what the elves called it, came to life. Lying never worked with him, and I was too exhausted to come up with one anyway. "Bad dream," I confessed.

"Same one or different?"

"Do you really have to ask?"

He sighed, setting his coffee down. "It's merely a nightmare," he insisted. "I think if you focus on something else aside from that vision, you'll stop seeing it every time you close your eyes."

"Right, and what would you like me to focus on instead?" I shot back. "The other visions, where I see everyone being torn to pieces?" I whispered harshly, not wanting the others to overhear me. "Or where I see fire destroying villages while the goblins dance over the bodies of the dead? Tell me, Alred, what would you like to me to focus on?"

He opened his mouth.

I raised my finger, pointing at him. "And so help

me if you say my training, I'm going to toss this scalding hot coffee in your face."

His mouth clamped shut, but his lips twitched. "Nice to see you have Garrick's temper."

"You never said anything about Garrick having anger issues."

Alred shifted on the wooden bench, avoiding my glance. "No, I didn't."

"Why?"

"I just didn't. Your temper's like his, though. He'd explode like a volcano when pushed too far. Nothing stood a chance when he reached that point," Alred told me quietly. "It was more toward the end of his life those episodes became normal."

I mulled over his words, tilting my head. "So, you're saying being the Historian changed him? The war changed him?"

"Nienna."

I laughed. "Wow. So much for those promises of not letting me turn into a heartless killer."

"I gave you my word. I won't let it happen."

"Yeah? And how are you going to stop it, huh? How?"

He sipped his coffee, ignoring my question. We sat in tense silence for a few minutes until I dropped the subject and went back to how his night went.

"Why do you care?" he countered after I asked him again about his impromptu date.

"I can't ask you about your personal life?"

"Nothing happened. Satisfied?" He pushed back from the table and marched to the doors. "If you're already up, we might as well get started on your training. Let's go."

"Oh, come on."

"Now, Nienna."

Rolling my eyes at his bossiness, I drained my coffee, snatched a biscuit and a few pieces of bacon, and hurried after Alred to the training courtyard. "Not sure what the point of all this is," I complained when he handed me a wooden practice sword a couple of minutes later. "I end up on my ass every time. You know, I think I'm not fit for the fighting aspect of this. Or coordinated enough."

"You need practice," he said, as he did every time I tried to get out of this side of my Historian training. Meditating with Thalia or Jurgis was more relaxing. Granted, I sucked at finding balance and being aware of my physical surroundings during a vision, but no one yelled at me during those sessions. Or scolded me. Or smacked me in the ass with a wooden sword when I repeatedly failed to reach a meditative state in the first place.

"Why don't you use guns?"

"Human technology, including guns, don't work in our world," he replied. "Magic disrupts them."

"Right, yeah, I totally knew that."

He stood at the ready and waited, his brow arched in the way that was starting to drive me crazy. Why did he have to be so handsome all the time? It was the scruffiness that had turned into a beard recently. It had to be. And his eyes, those dark green eyes with those gold flecks that glimmered whenever I annoyed him. His shirt stretched across his muscled chest, and I remembered all too easily how nice it was to be pressed against his body.

"Nienna."

"Hmm?"

"What are you thinking about?"

"Huh? Nothing, why?"

His lip twitched, but there was no smile. There hardly ever was these days. "You're blushing."

Great. I rolled my shoulders, shook out my hands, and planted my feet in the defensive stance he'd taught me the last few weeks. Ignoring his question, I nodded. I was ready to go, but he didn't move.

"What?"

He breathed out heavily through his nose,

scratching at his beard. The glint in his eyes said he wanted to say something. Instead, he shook his head, and without a sound, charged forward. I raised my wooden sword and blocked three strikes until he spun around and whacked me right in the ass with the broad side of his sword. I yelped, spinning around with a glare. He gave me a second to recover and came after me again.

Sweat dripped down my face, and my entire body screamed when the two suns reached their peak a few hours later. Alred bested me too many times to count, and with a yell, I threw myself at him, trying to tackle him. He easily side-stepped me, whacked me in the back this time.

I hit the stones with a grunt, fell over, and rolled onto my back, looking up at the clear blue sky while I panted. He stalked toward me, swinging his sword casually at his side. He opened his mouth for what I knew would be a lecture.

I twisted my body, wrapped my legs around his, and with a furious shout, rolled into him. He cursed and ended up on the stones right next to me.

"Ha."

He flipped back to his feet with no effort at all, holding out his hand for mine. "Nicely played. Think you earned a break."

"Just a break?"

I put my hand in his, biting my cheek to stop myself from reacting to how perfect holding his hand was. He pulled me to my feet, and I started to hand over the sword when a searing pain shot across my forehead. I gasped, falling forward, into Alred's arms.

Images appeared in my mind, and then I was standing in the gardens of Vel'Baram. There were no flowers left. The grounds, the flowerbeds, the trees, all were charred. The statues had been toppled over, and dead bodies were scattered about. These weren't soldiers. All of them were innocents. I tried to turn away, but the vision held me in its clutches, forcing me to see whatever atrocity the goblins had planned for the elves.

Slowly, I turned. The crackling of the fire consuming the towering trees cut through the thick silence. Banners I didn't recognize had been erected along the wall around Central Tower. Goblin clan sigils, maybe?

A howl had me whirling around in time to see goblins charging out of the gates, straight for me. A jagged blade rose high into the air, and when the bastard holding it prepared to cleave me in half, I was thrown out of the vision. I screamed, flailing get out of the way of the sword.

"Nienna? Look at me. Calm down. You're back."

I stilled as Alred cupped my face. I sagged in his arms, shivering. "Why do they have to feel so real sometimes?"

"It's how the visions work, sadly. What did you see?"

I tried to get up, but my knees buckled, and I sank to the ground with a muttered curse.

"Take a minute, let yourself recover." He pressed his hand to my forehead. A soothing coolness spread from his palm. It glowed briefly with his magic. The lines around his eyes crinkled with worry. "You're feverish."

"Happens every time. It's normal, right?"

"Yes, normal," he replied stiffly.

I tried to get up again, but when my legs wouldn't cooperate, he scooped me up and carried me away from the courtyard.

"You don't have to do this." My cheeks burned when his hands curled protectively around me. "Alred, seriously, I think I can walk now. Put me down. Please."

His jaw clenched, he set me on my feet, kept

one arm around my waist to support me, and we ambled the rest of the way inside. I took a deep breath and hated how even after we spent all morning training, he smelled of campfire and cedar. When I leaned into him, he slowed even more.

"Are you going to pass out?"

"No, sorry. I'm fine." I straightened and pushed away. "See? I'm good. I need to write down what I saw." After a few unsteady steps, I managed not to fall over. I hurried to my chambers. He followed but kept his distance. As we went, I told him what I saw, recalling the vivid details with a shudder. "But it's not happening soon."

"You're sure?"

"Yeah. I don't know how I know, but I do." I stilled outside my door. "There's something else. It might be nothing." I rubbed the back of my neck, a headache forming behind my eyes. "You know what, it's probably nothing. Never mind."

Alred caught my hand when I went to open the door. "Tell me."

I glanced at his hand on mine, and he swiftly pulled his away. "Fire," I said, the word coming out garbled. "There's been a fire in every vision I've had."

"It's a war," he said.

I shook my head. "Not like this. The fire, at first, I thought the fire was maybe my seeing things, but it's alive."

"What do you mean?"

His shoulders tensed, and his hand slipped to the dagger sheathed at his hip. These actions told me I was, in fact, not merely overreacting. "It aims for people, targets them. And it avoids the goblins. But fire can't do that, right? It's merely fire."

"Take the remainder of the day to rest," he said, ignoring my question. "I'll see you later."

"Alred?"

He paused with his back to me. "Rest, Nienna. You did well today." He stormed down the corridor, his boots echoing off the walls.

I slipped into my chambers, questioning what he was hiding from me when a rush of dizziness had me grabbing the doorframe. The same voice from this morning whispered through my thoughts, but the words were too quiet to hear.

The dizziness passed, and the voice faded.

I told myself it was nothing and hurried to write down my latest vision.

Chapter 2
ALRED

"Anything?"

Jurgis gave me an annoyed huff, not looking up from the massive book he currently had his nose buried in. "If you would give me more than five minutes to read, I might be able to give you an answer. And will you stop with the stomping? You're going to drive me insane."

I skidded to a stop. "Sorry."

"Why are you so anxious to know about dark magic anyway?"

"Something Nienna saw."

"She saw dark magic?" Jurgis exclaimed. "You're sure?"

"I don't know if it's dark magic, or what it is. I

simply need an answer to explain what she's seeing."

"What exactly did she tell you again?"

I ran my hands through my hair, tilting my head back while I studied the high domed ceiling of the old library. Lanterns hung from chains at various heights, flooding the room with a soft glow. The library was in the heart of the Central Tower; the curved walls were lined with books, scrolls, parchments, and documents collected throughout the centuries. Three sets of narrow stone steps led to the higher levels with twisting corridors and cramped rooms stuffed to the brim with texts. Jurgis, thankfully, was one of the few elves who understood the haphazard organized system of this place.

"She said the fire moved like it was alive. It targeted people. Fire didn't do that last time I checked."

"And she's sure that's what she saw?"

"In every vision. You and I both know if she's right, that it's not fire she's seeing."

Jurgis paled, his blue eyes flaring. "That's not simply dark magic. That's asking for an apocalypse. You have to tell the Seven."

"Not until I have something solid to tell them.

There could be some other fire creature that's not coming to my mind. Until I know for certain, I'd prefer not to cause panic."

"Has your gut instinct ever been wrong?" he questioned. "If you feel it's that ancient beast, then it most likely is. We knew the goblins were going to try to end us, but using magic like this? Letting such a monster free? It's crossing a line, even for them."

I agreed wholeheartedly with his words. Garrick had told Nienna there had to be a reason why the calling was showing her visions so far into the future. This had to be why. The goblins' attacks had slowed over the past five weeks. They hadn't stopped, but it was quieter than it had been in a long time.

"Find the answer for me, please," I told Jurgis. "Once you have, we'll speak to the Seven."

"And Nienna?"

I breathed out slowly. "I will tell her when she needs to know and not a second sooner."

Leaving him to his search, I prowled the corridors, avoiding the wing where Nienna's rooms were. My path took me to the gardens and beneath the willows. Even this far away, her distress and unease tried to drag me back inside. If I wasn't careful, I'd end up standing outside her door like I did most days. She had yet to catch me there, but one of these times, she would. This morning, the pull to her had been so strong it tore me out of a deep sleep and had me grabbing my sword until I realized she must've had another nightmare.

Her bad dreams weren't the only reason I was on edge every freaking day. Each time she had a vision, she was left weak, feverish, and hardly able to move. I'd studied the past Historians and had been with Garrick for twenty-seven years. Not one of them recorded suffering ill-effects from the visions.

And yet each time Nienna was sucked into one, I had to watch while her calling sapped her. The fever afterward lasted anywhere from a few minutes to a few hours. My magic soothed her and chased away the chill, so she stopped shivering, but nothing more. She was typically drained of energy and had to take it easy for the rest of the day. I came to dread each time her eyes glowed with a new vision, instead of being anxious to know what she saw. Part of me wished she'd never have to go through another one, if only to spare me from the stress.

"I haven't seen you look like that, well, ever."

I whipped around to find Trolian headed toward me. "I don't look like anything."

"You can tell that to the angry frown on your face. I heard Nienna had another vision."

"Did she share it with the Seven?"

"Yes, and like the last ones, they too believe it's in the far future, as she said." Trolian rested his shoulder against a willow tree. "Alred."

"What?" I snapped, continuing my pacing in the grass.

His brow rose, and he whistled. "Damn. I was wondering."

"Wondering what?" I muttered. "Nothing's going on."

"Really?"

I glared.

He shrugged.

"I think I'm allowed to be concerned when the Historian I'm tasked with protecting is not experiencing visions the way she should. And she's not sleeping. Nothing about Nienna's destiny is playing out as it ought to. Something's wrong, and I don't know what."

"And that's it? You're only worried because she's the Historian?"

I ceased my pacing and nodded. "What are you talking about?"

"Nothing. If you're so worried about her, why

don't you ease up a bit? You've been going non-stop with the training since we sent her friend back to the human world."

"There's no time to take a break. She has to be ready."

"Are you telling me you don't trust yourself to keep her safe?"

I placed my hand on the hilt of my dagger. "I will protect her with my life, but if she can't defend herself, and the enemy slips by me, kills me, I can't let anything happen to her."

"Still, a break would do you both some good."

Nienna was far behind where the other Historians had been in their training by this point, but Trolian was right. I needed time to understand her visions, and she could use a day off. "I might be pushing her too hard." Was that why the visions hit her so intensely? Wincing with guilt that I might be the reason for her distress, I muttered, "Maybe a couple of days off."

"You won't regret it."

I grunted, not sure I believed him.

"You going to tell me why Jurgis is frantically searching through the library and looking like he's about to lose it?"

"It's not a conversation I want to have here."

"How about we head to the tavern? You look like you could use a drink. Or several."

I debated leaving Nienna alone, but ale wasn't a bad idea. And I was working on keeping my distance from her when we weren't training or speaking with the Seven. However, the notion of kissing her rose in my mind at least once a day. Tamping down the urge was a fight I'd won so far. One of these days, I'd lose, and now was not the time to be starting a relationship that wasn't good for either of us.

Trolian and I left Central Tower behind and headed to the tavern. We'd barely sat down when an elf dragged out the chair beside me. She beamed at me, her dark hair flowing over her shoulders in waves that shimmered in the sunlight pouring through the stained-glass window.

"Hi," she said, her voice like silk. Her green, silk dress was elegant and clung to her like a second skin.

"Do I know you?" I asked, wondering if this was going to be like last night when Cellica randomly appeared at the tavern. And the time before that when another gorgeous elf sought me out.

She held out her hand, and on instinct, I shook

it. "Renna. And you are Alred, the Protector. That must be a fascinating duty, being there for the Historian all the time. Probably exhausting too. You look like you need to have a night of fun. How about I buy you an ale?"

"That's precisely what he needs," Trolian chimed in from across the table. I kicked him in the shin, and he cringed. "What? Let the pretty lady buy you an ale."

"I'm sorry, but I'm not exactly in the fun kind of mood right now."

She pouted, scooting closer. When she rested her hand on my arm, I gritted my teeth. Alright, not like last night. She was far pushier than Cellica had been.

"Listen," I said, picking up her hand and setting it on the table, "I'm not looking to date anyone or be with anyone."

"Oh, come on. I can change your mind. We can have a few ales, dance a bit. I think if you let yourself loosen up, you'll see that a woman in your life is exactly what you need."

I tensed at her words. "Did someone send you here?"

"What?" she said through her laughter. "No. Every woman in Vel'Baram knows who you are, and this is the longest you've stuck around. You're quite the wanted bachelor."

"Right. Sorry, love, but it's not going to happen."

She sighed, leaned in, and kissed my cheek. "If you change your mind, I'm usually here in the evenings. Feel free to find me."

I glared at Trolian as soon as she was gone.

"What? I didn't do anything," he muttered, but he grinned like an idiot.

"Are you doing this to me?"

"Doing what?"

"That's the fifth woman who's hit on me in the last two weeks. Whatever you think you're doing, it stops. Now. I'm not interested."

"Is that because you're interested in someone else?"

"No, it's because I can't afford to be distracted," I lied, because the woman I was interested in, I couldn't have. Shouldn't have.

Trolian nodded, still grinning.

"Did you want to hear about Jurgis or not?"

"Yes, no more talk of women. Tell me."

Keeping my voice low, I informed him of what Nienna had told me after her latest vision. As a captain, he was there for the meetings with the

Seven regarding what the Historian had seen, but I'd doubted Nienna would mention the fire. She believed it was merely a coincidence. When I reached the part about the flames being alive, his blue eyes darkened like the ocean during a storm, and he cursed.

"Now, do you understand my concern?" I asked.

"It can't be that," he muttered. "They wouldn't dare."

"Maybe not all of them, but if Ioc is vying for control of the clans and he lets his sons make the decisions? They might not care what chaos they're about to unleash on Kenzu'grote."

"It can't be controlled. It would destroy them once it finished with us."

We drank our ale in silence, the noise of the tavern setting my teeth on edge. I drained my mug, paid, and told Trolian I'd see him later. I hoped a walk would clear my head, but all it did was give me too much time to think about what these visions meant.

I wanted an end to the war, but what Nienna saw wasn't the end I thought was possible. The first vision Nienna had, the nightmare she experienced every night, was that where we'd end up? Was that really the end of everything?

Without meaning to, I ended my walk outside her door, pulled to her as I always was by her fear. I raised my hand to knock, but there was nothing I could say to make that fear go away.

Quickly, I backed off and went to the courtyard to train with the other soldiers. Wearing myself out to the point of exhaustion so I'd sleep wouldn't be a bad thing right now.

*****

I sent a message to Nienna's rooms late last night, letting her know training for today was canceled. It proved to be anything but a relaxing day for me, and I checked on Jurgis, who was hidden behind a stack of books in the library. He thought he'd found something that might explain the fire monster rampaging through Nienna's visions.

I didn't get to hear about it. He shoved me out the door, saying I was nothing but a distraction. He slammed the doors shut in my face, and I was left to wander the grounds, mind racing with what we were possibly walking into.

"Alred," Thalia called, and I turned to find her

and two members of the Seven coming toward me. "You look terribly deep in thought."

I bowed to Thalia. Galan and Dain shook my hand. They were brothers from the Goldlance court. Their gold irises constantly shifted through several hues of gold and copper then back again, much like the sun. They stood as tall as I did and once upon a time had been soldiers before they were summoned to be members of the Seven.

"Something troubles you," Dain stated with his deep baritone voice.

"When doesn't something trouble me," I replied.

"Does this have anything to do with why Jurgis is in the library?" Thalia asked.

"I was going to come to you once I had answers, but if you'd like to know now, then we can talk."

"No," Galan said, his voice the same as his brother's. "If we all need to know, it can wait. How is the Historian's training going?"

"As well as can be expected, considering where she started. I assume Thalia has told you of her progress or attempt at progress on controlling the visions." Nienna had shared her frustrations with me several times about how she had yet to reach a successful meditative state. I hesitated, clasping my hands behind my back, and shook my head. "I'm sorry, it's nothing."

"Alred, if you think it's something, then I doubt it's nothing," Thalia commented.

I hated to add more worries to their shoulders, but it was my duty to inform them of any and all issues with the Historian. "Her visions leave her weak, so weak she can hardly stand. And she's feverish afterward. I've never heard of a Historian having such problems. I certainly never saw them with Garrick."

"She's in the first stages of her calling. It's only been a little over a month," Galan said. "She's adjusting to the power of the tome. I would give her time. Her being half-human could also be complicating the situation, but I wouldn't worry yet."

The elf's words did nothing to soothe my troubled mind. Galan and Dain walked on, but Thalia lingered behind, a knowing look in those silver-blue eyes of hers. She motioned down the path.

"Why don't we take a walk?" she suggested. "You're sure there's nothing else bothering you?"

"Aside from what Jurgis is researching, no, nothing."

"I don't know why you insist on lying to me."

I smiled. "Can you blame me?"

"I'm not exactly one to gossip. You know me better than that, I would hope." We made it a few steps when she spoke again. "So, Trolian tells me you're quite a hit with the women lately."

My head fell back, and I grunted, irritated. "I don't understand it."

"You're an attractive elf who's single, and you hold one of the most respected positions in all of Kenzu'grote. What's not to understand?"

"But why now? I've been in Vel'Baram for nearly thirty years. It's as if someone's telling them I'm looking for a relationship." I stopped cold and cursed. "That's precisely what someone's doing."

"What, trying to set you up? I could think of worse things to be done to you."

"It's not what I want," I replied quietly.

I'd thought it was Trolian behind the matchmaking, but he knew me too well. I wouldn't simply give in and start dating some random elf who came up to me. I continued walking, Thalia with me, and we turned the corner in the gardens.

The hedges parted, and Nienna's laugh struck my ears.

I glanced up to spot where she and Trolian were talking, across the flowerbeds. No, not talking. Flirting. Openly flirting. He handed her a flower, and she took it with a smile that lit up her green eyes.

I looked away, storming off the other direction.

"Ah, so that's what's got you all twisted and turned around," Thalia said, staying with me.

"What?"

"Nienna."

I tripped on a small rock and promptly righted myself. "If you mean I'm worried, as her Protector, then yes, you'd be right."

"No, I mean you have feelings for her." I picked up the pace until Thalia grabbed my arm, tugging me to a stop. "Alred, there's nothing in the rules that say a Protector can't be with the Historian. Why not simply tell her?"

"I can't afford to be distracted, and if I give in to these feelings, that's what I will be. Her life depends on my staying focused."

"Yes, because you're so focused right now."

I opened my mouth then shut it, hanging my head. "She's pushing me away, too."

"Why would she do that?"

"I have several theories, but I'm not about to ask her because it can't happen."

"You're the only one saying that," Thalia pointed out. "We might live for hundreds of years, but our lives are still limited. We only have so much time to enjoy them and be happy, genuinely happy. We may never see the end of this war. It could kill us tomorrow or next week. We can't know for certain. But," she added, squeezing my arm until I looked into her eyes, "I plan on making the most of every moment I have, and that means not hiding behind my sense of duty. If you want to be with her, then tell her before it's too late." She gave my cheek a hard pat and strolled away, her violet dress trailing on the stones.

Eventually, I returned to my chambers, not trusting myself to stay away from Nienna. I pictured her talking with Trolian and found myself analyzing the scene I'd witnessed. He'd flirted with her. Had she flirted back? Maybe I was merely seeing things.

"Not that it matters," I spat at my reflection. "She can flirt with whoever she likes."

I gripped the edge of the vanity as a jealous voice whispered through my mind that she seemed content to only push me away, but not Trolian. I stalked around my room, unable to stop picturing her with him. I'd been hard on her, yes, but the times we kissed, I know she experienced the same feelings as I did. The same connection that went beyond our bonds as Historian and Protector.

Granted, for the few weeks after, I pretended it didn't happen. That didn't mean I felt nothing for her. This was why I hated the notion of caring for someone. Loving them. It was too complicated. Too disruptive. Not that I loved Nienna. It wasn't possible, not this soon.

When evening came around, and I joined the others in the hall for dinner, I watched for Nienna and Trolian, determined to find out if she was returning the flirting. I told myself to stop acting like a lovesick child and let it be.

Sulking over my food, I ignored the conversations around me until Nienna's voice made my ears pricked. I found her easily, and right beside her was Trolian. They sat at the other long table, excitedly talking about something. I bit my tongue and winced. I was draining my goblet of wine when someone sat down beside me. All I spotted was the trailing long, blond hair.

I hunched my shoulders. "Not in the mood for your flirting. Go away."

"Trolian was right; you are in a foul mood."

I glanced up to see Commander Kali Leafsun

sitting beside me, smirking. "Sorry. Thought you were someone else."

"Someone trying to flirt with you?"

"It's a long story."

"Oh, I was told. You're the talk of Vel'Baram. Someone said you're currently available. Wonder who that was?"

I poured more wine for myself and filled her goblet, too. "I have no idea, but whoever it is, I'm going to kill them. I'm not available, and the endless stream of flirting is going to drive me insane. I have enough crazy to deal with."

"I'll bet you do."

Nienna laughed, and Trolian leaned in closer to her.

When his hand rested on hers, the fork in my hand didn't stand a chance. The metal bent with a tiny spurt of magic escaping my control, and Kali's brow arched. I dropped the bent utensil, pushed my plate away, and satisfied myself with wine.

"Never knew you to be the jealous type."

"I'm not."

"Tell that to the poor fork you just killed."

I gave the fork a heated glare. "She can talk to whoever she wants. I don't care."

"You can say that all you want, but you look like you're about to go over there and murder Trolian."

"Can we talk about something else? Anything else?"

She held up her hands. "Fine, be an idiot. What do I care?"

"Kali—" The hair on the back of my neck stood, and a faint pain shot across my forehead. I leapt to my feet.

Nienna's eyes glazed over. The gold flecks glowed, and she was sucked into a vision.

Trolian and the elves around her froze. The rest of the hall fell silent.

For a second, she seemed to be alright, then her mouth fell open, and she screamed.

I sprinted around the tables toward her. She toppled back off the bench and into my arms. I held her while she thrashed violently, screaming as if she was being physically attacked.

Trolian and Kali knelt next to me as we struggled to keep Nienna from hurting herself on the stone floor. Her back arched, and she threw her head to the side, wincing in pain. I held her head gently but firmly and managed to get her onto my lap so at least she wouldn't bash her skull in.

The glow of her eyes brightened, and she let

out one more bloodcurdling scream. Her body sagged, and she went still.

Panic struck me. "Nienna?"

She gasped for air. The glow dimmed in her eyes, and they shut.

"Nienna, come on. Open your eyes." I gave her shoulders a gentle shake. "Damn it, woman, look at me."

Her breathing calmed, and too slowly, her eyes fluttered open. "Alred?" She tried to sit up.

Gently, I stopped her. "Give yourself a minute."

She was burning up but shivered. I glanced at Kali and Trolian. They rose and called for everyone to clear the hall and for someone to bring Jurgis. Thalia was the only member of the Seven currently present. She stayed behind, giving Nienna a worried look, and sat on the floor beside us.

"Fire. There was so much fire, and it had a face. I swear it had a face," Nienna whispered. "I saw it. I need to write it down." She tried to get up again, but I refused to let her move. I pressed my palm to her forehead, attempting to ease the fever away as I'd been doing. She stared at me, her brow wrinkling. "I'm fine, I promise."

I scowled, shaking my head. "I don't care if you think you're fine. You're not moving yet."

She blinked and finally glanced around. "Wait, how did I get on the floor?"

"You had a fit," I explained. "Whatever you saw, it had you screaming like you were being torn apart."

She gulped, and I smoothed her hair from her face. She reached up, catching my hand, and squeezed it.

"I've got you," I tried to reassure her.

She was flushed from the fever, with terror in her gaze. "I was dying," she whispered, and my heart pounded with my rising anxiety. "The fire, it came right for me. It tore through a line of soldiers, and then it was all around me. I couldn't get away, and everyone was dying…" She scrunched her eyes shut. "I can still smell their skin burning."

"You can write it all down in a moment. Rest."

She closed her eyes and slowly relaxed. Thalia said she would send someone to fetch the tome.

Jurgis arrived a short moment later, his gaze heavy with fear. He nodded. His expression said it all.

Mentally, I cursed.

Evidently, he found what he was looking for, which meant we were all in far more trouble than I'd first realized.

I hope you enjoyed *The Librarian*!
Get more of Ciara's books here!

Sign up for Ciara's Newsletter to find out about
new releases
Click the link below
Newsletter
or put the following in your browser window:

landing.mailerlite.com/webforms/landing/b1c5z2

www.ingramcontent.com/pod-product-compliance
Lightning Source LLC
Chambersburg PA
CBHW051951150726
47999CB00004B/1339